P9-CMX-755

# MONSTER'S CHEF

ALSO BY JERVEY TERVALON

**FICTION**

*UNDERSTAND THIS*

*DEAD ABOVE GROUND*

*ALL THE TROUBLE YOU NEED*

*LITA*

*LIVING FOR THE CITY*

**NONFICTION**

*THE COCAINE CHRONICLES* (COEDITOR WITH GARY PHILLIPS)

*GEOGRAPHY OF RAGE:*
*REMEMBERING THE LOS ANGELES RIOTS OF 1992* (EDITOR)

# MONSTER'S CHEF

A NOVEL

JERVEY TERVALON

Amistad
*An Imprint of* HarperCollins*Publishers*
www.amistadbooks.com

This is a work of fiction. The characters, incidents, and dialogues are products of the author's imagination and are not to be construed as real. Any resemblance to actual persons, living or dead, is entirely coincidental.



HarperCollins books may be purchased for educational, business, or sales promotional use. For information, please e-mail the Special Markets Department at SPsales@harpercollins.com.

Recipes courtesy of Lester Walker and Malcolm Livington II

FIRST EDITION

Library of Congress Cataloging-in-Publication Data has been applied for.

ISBN 978-0-06-231620-2

14 15 16 17 18 OV/RRD 10 9 8 7 6 5 4 3 2 1

For my wife:
my love and my first reader,
Jinghuan Liu Tervalon

献给我妻子:
我的爱人,我的第一个读者
刘静环

# MONSTER'S CHEF

## SUNNY ORRECHIETTE WITH COLLARDS AND BREAD CRUMBS

SERVES 4

3 cups turkey wing stock
1 pound collard greens
5 tablespoons extra-virgin olive oil (EVOO), plus more as needed for eggs and drizzling
1 cup coarse fresh bread crumbs
3 cloves garlic, roasted and minced
1½ shallots, peeled and "brunoised"
Salt and freshly ground black pepper
3 tablespoons unsalted butter
Four 1-inch-thick slices cured slab bacon
¼ teaspoon crushed red pepper flakes
1 pound orrechiette
4 free-range chicken eggs
¾ cup grated Parmigiano

In a large pot, bring the stock to a boil. Working in batches, cook the collards in the stock until just tender, about 6 minutes. Using tongs, transfer the collards to a medium sheet pan and let cool. Set the stock aside in its pot. Squeeze out excess liquid from the collards; chop the leaves and finely chop the stems; set aside.

Heat 3 tablespoons EVOO in a small skillet over medium heat. Add the bread crumbs and cook, stirring often, until the crumbs begin to brown, about 4 minutes. Add one-third of the garlic and one-third of the shallots and cook, stirring often, until the bread crumbs are golden, about 3 minutes. Season with salt and black pepper and transfer to a paper-towel-lined sizzle plate; let cool.

Heat the butter and 2 tablespoons EVOO in a large heavy pot over low-medium heat. Add the chopped bacon, red pepper flakes, and the remaining garlic and shallots; cook about 2 minutes. Add the reserved collards and ½ cup stock. Cook, stirring often, until the collards are warmed through, about 4 minutes. Season with salt and pepper. Set aside.

Meanwhile, bring the reserved stock to a boil; add the pasta and cook, stirring occasionally, until al dente. Drain, reserving 1 cup of the stock.

In a small skillet over medium heat, warm some additional EVOO, add the eggs, and cook until the egg white coagulates. Season with salt and ground black pepper, cover for 30 seconds until the eggs are not runny, and set aside.

Add the pasta and ½ cup pasta liquid to the collard mixture and stir to coat. Return to medium heat and continue stirring, adding more liquid as needed, until the sauce coats the pasta. Mix in the cheese and ½ cup bread crumbs; toss to combine.

Divide the pasta among bowls; drizzle with oil; and top with the remaining bread crumbs and the eggs, sunny side up. Drizzle with a little more EVOO.

# CHAPTER ONE

SILENCE, SOLITUDE, AND BREATHABLE AIR, that's all I wanted, not exactly a miracle, but I guess this nightmare of a job is what I deserve. I'm the cook; what goes on beyond the locked door of this bungalow is not my concern. I turn up music, keep lights burning all through the night.

Safe.

No one cares about the cook, that's what I count on. I keep the door locked, and I try not to leave, not anymore, not after dark.

Cold.

This bungalow is torture even in spring. No matter how much wood I toss into the barely functional woodstove, heat slips away through the walls like mice when I turn on the lamp. I came with few clothes—two white tunics and a couple of thick sweaters, jeans and T-shirts. I wear both sweaters to bed, all the socks I can fit on. Coldest I've been is spring in the mountains of Santa Ynez. Some nights I can't bring myself to get out of bed to use the toilet, just grit my teeth and endure until I can't stand it.

You'd think somebody as rich as Monster would insulate these bungalows, might have some idea that his employees are suffering. Even so I should have been better prepared, should have known, paid more attention to what I was getting myself into. A man of Monster's stature spends his time plotting world conquest, opening a Planet Monster in Bali or something fantastic, not worrying about the frigid temperature of an employee's bungalow. Maybe that's why the last chef quit, fingers so numb she couldn't dice.

Another glass of 2005 Rutherford Hillside Reserve Cabernet and I'm still feeling the cold, though it's not as sharp. I told myself I was through with Twelve Step anything; I can't feel good about getting wasted. Numb is good and warm, but numb turns sour, numb gets you arrested, numb gets you a judge deciding what's best for you, and I can't stand to live through another diversion program. I pour the rest of the wine down the drain. I swore to myself that I would get high on life only, and leave killing myself a little each day alone.

I KNOW THESE EXTENSIVE, meandering grounds well, but on a moonless night it's almost impossible to stay on the trail. A step in the wrong direction and you're in the middle of scrub brush and poison oak that rib all sides of Monster's estate. Easily enough you can end up blindly wandering in the wilderness among coyotes, black bear, mountain lions, whatever.

See.

You must walk away from the light into the darkness.

The other direction isn't an option; the closer one gets to the big house, the more likely the lights will go on, blinding lights that'll make you feel like a frog ready to be scooped into a sack. Then you'll hear the sound of the heavy steps of Security as they converge, shouting commands. It's been worse since some nameless stalker managed, after repeated attempts, to sneak into Monster's Lair on some psychotic mission. Someone, maybe even Monster, came up with "Lair" as the name for this place. Heard it's trademarked and he's going to use it for his next CD, whenever he gets that done. Clever, I guess, but I don't know. Supposedly, he's been having a hell of a time—the music won't flow at Monster's Lair. Maybe it's the name; it's not conducive to creativity. Try telling someone you live and work at Monster's Lair and they laugh and ask, *With that lunatic? How is that? What kind of craziness goes on there?*

I can't answer.

They never did catch the trespasser, supposedly a loser from Monster's past who's plagued him since long before he built the Lair playland. I used to enjoy my nightly walks, but that was before enhanced lighting and the dogs. Security lets them run the grounds to get the lay of the land.

Once, I saw Monster walking alone in the middle of a pack of trained attack dogs like he was fucking Saint Francis of Assisi. Security trailed behind him, skulking near the bushes, maintaining that illusion of privacy he demands. The dogs smelled me, and though I was trying to back away from the encounter, too late, they charged forward, frothing and churning sod. Monster looked for a moment like he had no idea who I was, the man hired to cook for him and his family. I raised my walking stick to bash a dog before the others mauled me, but an impulse of self-preservation kicked in and I shouted my name just as the dogs charged.

"It's me, Gibson! The cook!" Security shouted something in German to the dogs, which stopped midstride. I heard Monster's voice, high and nasal, a near whine. "Oh, you scared me."

"Sorry," I said, and hurried on in the opposite direction. I caught a glimpse of him in the moonlight, bundled in a parka, though that night the temperature was mild, walking with hands clasped behind his back, serenely in thought. Security caught up and escorted me back to my bungalow, which was more and more a jail cell and less the attractive perk of a rent-free cottage in the beautiful mountains to compensate for a modest salary. Security looked me in the eye and told me to watch it, don't forget who pays the bills.

"Monster does," I said, nodding to show, even if Security wasn't buying it, that I was a team player. It didn't go well. He looked for a second as though he thought I might be jerking his chain, then turned to go, but not before jotting something down in a small gray notebook that I'm sure was a notation scheduling another background check. I didn't mind.

When you work for someone with great wealth, you learn quickly that you really do serve him. You learn to be blind, deaf, and dumb if that's what they need.

Monster needs all of that.

Sometimes I see things that don't add up, that make me nervous. I wanted isolation, but not like this. The night sky has too many stars; the moon hangs like a gaudy lantern illuminating a path to my bungalow. I've never felt so alone. I know what goes on there, behind those hedges, those walls, gates, and sensors.

He's a monster and every day I serve him.

I'M NOT INCLINED toward depression; upbeat and all of that is how folks describe me, but that was because of the drugs.

Married, living on the Lower East Side in a nice co-op, part owner of Euro Pane, a restaurant with witty, angular (the publicist came up with that), Puglia-inspired cuisine that people wanted to spend good hard cash on—you'd think I'd have been more than happy, but in truth it was too much for me. Maybe I couldn't stand prosperity, and with things going so well I knew my luck couldn't continue; something would give and I'd find myself flat on my face. Instead of waiting, I went for it, leaped for the pipe and returned to a long-dormant cocaine habit. If I needed to make an excuse, more to myself than anyone else, I could offer that the restaurant was overwhelming, and I needed relief from the day-to-day, week-to-week, month-to-month relentless grind, the kind where you wake yourself with the sound of your own teeth grinding. Yeah, it's the kind of stress that makes a man long for a hit off a crack pipe.

Ten years ago, when I indulged in smoking a little cocaine, I handled it. But now was different. Then it was about staying up to dawn for the second day, clubbing until I was sick of the whole idea of clubbing. Working and playing, trying to have everything, and it worked until I couldn't stand living like that. I gave it up, put down the pipe and cocaine easily, proved to myself that cocaine didn't have me by the balls. Suddenly I noticed I had so much more money in my bank account, and then I met Elena, fell in love, and that was that. It really was a good thing, and I handled it smoothly, so smoothly that I had it in the back of my mind that I could do it again. It wouldn't be no thing. But I guess shit has a way of catching up to you after a while. My addiction was like a cancer cell, dormant; I was kicking it until the conditions were right. Probably the truth is I don't have the same discipline or constitution. I'm not that young man who could do that, keep it going, burning myself out in every direction. Soon enough I lost the restaurant to my partner and my wife found my fucked-up, vulgar habit reason enough to leave me. I don't blame her. She didn't marry a fiend, I became one, and it just took time for me to discover it, my inclination toward self-immolation. I call it that, the suicidal impulse to consume myself with a Bic lighter. I'd see myself burned out, gone, a neat pile of ashes, but that's more acceptable to my imagination than the vision of myself as a pathetic cracked-lip panhandler, a martyr to the pipe. Maybe I wanted to fail, see how far I could fall.

Far and hard—Lucifer had nothing on me. Being broke is like having a bloody mouth and loose teeth, and there's not a thing you can do about it except stand it.

How does that song go? "You spell New York with a nickel, dime, and fork, cocaine, Jim," something like that. But I'm not judging. I thought I could master my high. I wish I'd had the courage to stay in the city, for everyone to see me living in a halfway house, trying to reassemble the remaining shards of my self-respect. What if I ran into her, Elena, my wife? It's wrong to say that, we're more divorced than married, but far as I'm concerned she still is. Funny how memory works; when you don't fill it with anything new, it replays what maybe you don't want replayed. My mind replays Elena.

Short, with hair like the blackest ink, strong legs and ass, a delicate face; almost Japanese, like a geisha in an ukiyo-e print; and passionate about love and making money and everything else, passionate about hating me. I still love her, though it's hopeless to think she'll ever love me again. I want her back more than the restaurant, a reputation, everything, but it will never happen, not in this life and not in the next. Left with nothing other than to lie in bed and think about what I've done, hurt the woman I love and lost her; didn't consider the consequences back then, didn't have bouts of guilt, didn't consider anything. It was about me, about what's good for the head. You know, the head. A selfish bitch, that's the truth about me. About me, that's all it ever was; my love was a fraud, my professionalism a joke, my self-respect delusion.

And I'll never get it back. You'd think I'd find the courage to do something dramatic, maybe kill myself or find God, but no, I indulged in self-pity while waiting to be saved from myself.

ELENA PARTIED HARD, but you know it didn't get to her. She did it all—heroin, coke, ecstasy—but when she was through with it, she was through. Maybe it was yoga or the Stair-Master, but mostly it was because Elena wanted a baby, and she's that type of person. So directed and focused that she didn't stop to think that the rest of the world, and by that I mean me, might not be able to live the way she managed to. It took forever for her to see that I had a weakness. Never raised an eyebrow when, after sharing a few lines, I excused myself to go to the bathroom to do a few more lines. She even laughed when she saw me fumbling to put everything away, hastily brushing white powder from my face, more evidence of my lack of control. It was funny in a way. She should have noticed that I was craving, fiending, whatever you want to call it. I had started my downward journey, my decline; in it to win it, a new life consisting of one long sustained need to stay high.

My recollection of conversations with Elena replay themselves and I listen to myself ruin my marriage.

*"We're four months behind on the mortgage?" Elena asked.*

*"No, I don't think it's that far along. Maybe two months," I replied.*

*"What happened to the money? We'll lose the apartment."*

*"Things got away from me. I'm sure we can put something together to work this out."*

*"What are the chances of that happening?"*

*I shrugged. I didn't want to lie to her.*

*"Do you know what you're doing to us, the fact that you can't control yourself? Why don't you admit it, stop being in denial?"*

*She looked at me with smoldering black eyes.*

*"You need professional help."*

*"I don't have that kind of problem."*

*"You're forcing me—no, you're giving me no choice but to leave you."*

*"Come on," I said. "We'll work this out."*

*This time she laughed bitterly.*

*"Sure we will," she said, but we both knew that was a lie.*

AFTER THAT SHE MOVED IN with a friend and refused to talk to me, but that particular humiliation didn't sting much because later that week at court I pled guilty and was sentenced to nine months in a minimum-security prison.

In some sense I was happy to be going, having done enough damage to my self-esteem that I wanted to crawl away into a corner and wait for the room to stop spinning. And, when it did, I woke up to the humiliation of getting processed, prepared, prepped, and more to go to the place to do my time. My only regret is that I wasn't high during that humiliation.

The days inside prison weren't totally unpleasant; they had a good enough library, and I spent time lifting weights for the first time in my life. That's it, I thought, do positive things for yourself while incarcerated and avoid being raped, but in a minimum-security prison the only thing I had to worry about was getting athlete's foot in the shower.

I had hoped to hear from Elena at some point, but after months passed, I began to wonder if I would. After I was released and moved to the halfway house, she wrote and said she would be coming to visit for me to sign divorce papers—that I later learned she didn't file.

I tried not to allow those words to rise to the surface. I waited with far too much hope on that moment when she'd appear at the door of the halfway house to be shown inside by one of the workers, who would sign her in and bring me out to sit across from her on the worn couch. Me, smiling stupidly, thinking, feverishly hoping, that her seeing me again would jar something loose and make her want to forget about the divorce. It was what it was, paperwork.

She wore all black. Tight wool skirt and a sweater that looked good on her. But she kept her arms crossed, probably remembering how much I liked her small breasts.

I don't think she ever smiled. Talked to me about some issues, bankruptcy, insurance policy. Nothing I was interested in; I was interested in her, but that was dead.

I was dead to her.

She took it personally, like I had rejected her for cocaine, but it wasn't like that.

How did she ask it?

"How could you be so fucking stupid? Getting yourself arrested buying heroin on the subway?"

I shrugged. I guess if it were the first time, she might

have been able to excuse it, but it wasn't. To this day I don't know how stupid I am. I don't think I've plumbed the depths of my stupidity, and when I do, I plan to get back to her. I'll have charts and graphs, a PowerPoint demonstration. I ruined my life, I know that; the last thing I wanted to do was betray her, but I was good at that too, excelled at it even.

ASHA, THE WOMAN who ran the halfway house, realized I could cook South Asian. Being Gujarati, she was surprised that I made a better *bhindi*-spiced eggplant than her mother. She discovered that I could stay in seclusion in a sweltering kitchen, cooking meals for the dozen or so parolees who lived at the halfway house. I labored away in silent grief, working with old vegetables, day-old bread, not much meat (which pleased Asha because she didn't like the smell), some chicken, beans, lots of beans. I came up with meal after meal through backbreaking efficiency and invention. When I wasn't cooking, I cleaned. I scoured that kitchen, boiled water, added cupfuls of caustic soap, cleaned the filthy ceiling, cleaned everything. Made it spotless, and kept it that way as long as I was there, my six months climbing out of the black hole of my life.

Cooking and cleaning and not thinking were meditative balms. I hated when thoughts slithered in on their own and had their way with me. Grief caught me slipping; I needed to see her; thought of leaving, blowing the whole thing off, my contract with the halfway house staff, to make a run to see her, force her to listen to me. But then I'd go to prison and I had sense enough to know I didn't want that.

Maybe I might have tried, maybe prison would have been worth it, if I could get her to listen to me, but I had no words left to beg with. I was out of prayers and I was sick of lighting candles to the patron saint of hopeless causes.

She was gone; maybe here, probably in some other city.

"It's for the best," my caseworker said when I confessed why I wouldn't talk in therapy.

"It's not about the drugs. It's about losing my wife."

"Drugs are why you lost her. You drove her away."

I cried then, in front of that fool. I stopped talking to him after that. Before that I felt like maybe he was okay. I was wrong. Up until that moment, I didn't want to do cocaine again. I really was through with it. And then the cravings started and the fiction that kept me alive, that the drug did me and that I didn't do the drug, fluttered away and I couldn't hide from my fiendishness.

Trying to avoid contact with my fellow losers at the halfway house, I took to mincing cloves of garlic, like garlic would keep everyone at bay, as though they were vampires, vampires that suck smoke instead of blood. It worked; they kept their distance, except for Asha; I was her reclamation project. I accepted her good intentions, but I didn't want to be drawn out or in, or anywhere. I wanted to stay lost. Alone would be good, but I had to get with the Twelve Step program, show requisite progress to get these people out of my life. Still, Asha was pleasant and charming, with big, luminous eyes that were easy to look into. Good thing she didn't go for men because our friendship would have been much more complicated. Finally, I explained a little about myself, and so when she came into the kitchen with this look on her face, I knew I had probably said too much.

"What's wrong?"

"You! I read about you."

"What? That I'm a fuckup? You already knew that."

She shook her head.

"Yeah, I made a mess of what most people think was a promising career."

"Don't you miss that life? Running that restaurant, cooking?"

"I don't know. I guess I do."

"My girlfriend works for this famous entertainer. She says he needs a chef."

I raised an eyebrow in spite of myself.

"I wouldn't get past the interview," I said.

"She's crazy about me and listens to what I have to say. If you're interested, you'd have a shot."

"I'll think about it," I said without a hint of enthusiasm. I wondered why she wanted to go out of her way for me; she was more than clever enough to notice I was a fuckup. It had to be her nature, trusting and giving, and maybe a bit naive, coupled with being smart about people and hard-nosed about the everyday affairs of running the halfway house. I guess that's what you need in her line of work, skills that contradict one another. Strange how a woman, young and attractive, would choose social work—running a halfway house must be like hanging around unflushed toilets all day—when she could choose so many more attractive occupations. Maybe she wanted to be a Hindu Mother Teresa and if she could drag me back to respectability, she'd be one giant step closer to sainthood.

THE INTERVIEW WAS AT THE TRUMP PLAZA, at this overblown, overhyped restaurant that only idiots thought anything of.

Bridget, Asha's girlfriend, was a thin blonde who wore a short skirt, though I could see the first flurries of snow falling from the gray sky.

"I hate New Jersey," I said.

Bridget laughed. I didn't mean for it to be funny.

"So, you had that cute restaurant in the Village."

I smiled. "I don't know about it being so cute," I said.

"I loved that place," she said.

"I did too, but not enough."

"Really? How so?"

"When I think about it, maybe I didn't care for it."

Bridget nervously tapped a fork against her water glass.

"Gibson is a fantastic cook," Asha said. She glanced at me and probably could tell I was near tears.

"What happened?" Bridget asked.

I shrugged, and Asha took over. She leaned over and began to whisper to Bridget. Asha wore this loose-fitting, burnished-gold tunic; her dark skin and hair looked even richer against the paleness of Bridget's skin and hair. As she whispered, whatever resistance Bridget had toward me faded. Bridget was totally smitten with Asha, and when she took her hand, she was transported.

I was almost embarrassed to see how much she was taken with Asha.

"Listen," Bridget said, loud enough for me to hear. "I'll tell you the bottom line. We have a hard time getting quality people up on the mountain."

"Why is that?" I asked.

"It's a tough job, the type of job for a particular person who wants to be in a beautiful place and needs privacy. It's very private there."

"You mean isolated?"

"I call it very private. You can call it what you like."

"Isolated. I don't mind isolation. I don't mind it at all."

"Do you know who Lamont Stiles is?"

I shook my head.

"You've heard of Monster Stiles?" Bridget asked.

"He's that singer?"

"He doesn't do much of that anymore. He's more of a producer, with three acts at the top of the charts. Everything he touches is bling; his clothing line made millions last year, and this year it's expected to double in sales."

"When you say 'bling,' you mean . . . ?"

"Beyond priceless. You had to have heard of that expression."

"Yeah, but I never used it."

She looked at me as if she had already made up her mind about me.

"So, Mr. Stiles needs a chef?" I asked.

"He prefers to be called Monster. He fancies himself the monster of music, of cutting-edge fashion, of life."

"Monster it is."

Bridget laughed. "I like how direct you are."

Her face hardened. We were going to get down to it. "You need to understand how this works. If you repeat this to anyone, I'll get fired and you'll get sued."

I laughed. "Listen, I'm on parole. If I don't jump through hoops, I go to jail."

She nodded and smiled at me after Asha patted her hand.

"This might be hard to believe, but many people aren't comfortable on the mountain. It takes a special person, someone who really enjoys quiet and his own company. The perfect candidate for this job loves nature, because that's where you are, in the clouds. It's God's most beautiful, pristine country. That's what Monster loves about it, he's above it all, but people get lonely for their families, for life outside of the Lair. Plus, well, Monster is demanding. He says that about himself."

"How so?"

Bridget sucked her teeth. "You haven't heard all of that rubbish about him?"

"No, I really don't keep up with the music scene."

"He made all those bubblegum pop songs. You got to wonder about people like that," Asha muttered. "And he had that pet koala hanging around his neck."

"He's got rid of the koala, that was a big mistake," Bridget said, with perfect seriousness.

"I'm not sure about this. What do people say about him? Is there any truth to it?"

Bridget laughed. "I'm not going to go into it. People say all kinds of things about him. You'd think he bathes in the blood of little boys, that kind of *National Enquirer* bullshit."

"What do you think of him?"

"Well, it's hard to explain," she said, softly, as though she was wary of being overheard. "Monster isn't really someone I see a lot of. He is a great employer in that he's very generous. But mostly he's on the road or holed up in the Lair—that's what he wants us to call it. It's really his encampment, the inner grounds of his mansion and the gardens where most staff aren't allowed. I think that's how those horrible stories of Monster get out. Disgruntled former employees spread rumors when they really don't know what goes on in the Lair. Anyway, if you're really interested, I'll fly you out to interview. Asha can come with you. I'll show you Solvang, and there's this wonderful little Danish bakery. You'll love the pastries."

"I'm not sure of what he wants. Will I be his personal chef, or will I be running the kitchen for everyone there?"

"You know, I couldn't tell you at this point. With Monster you go with the flow; he'll fill in the blanks, he always does."

Bridget shrugged and put her head on Asha's shoulder.

Business was done for the evening.

## ENGLISH PEA SOUP WITH MORELS

SERVES 4

4 teaspoons unsalted butter, plus more as needed for the shallot and garlic

3 cipolline onions, peeled and "brunoised"

1 small carrot, peeled and cut into ½-inch diamonds

2 teaspoons Maldon salt or flaky sea salt

½ cup dry white wine

Five-finger pinch of chopped tarragon leaves, plus torn leaves for finishing

4 cups smoked ham hock broth, plus more for deglazing

Two 10-ounce packages premium frozen baby peas

Extra-virgin olive oil (EVOO)

4 tablespoons crème fraîche

1 shallot, peeled and "brunoised"

1 clove garlic, minced

Freshly ground black pepper

1 pound fresh morel mushrooms

Put 4 teaspoons butter in a large lidded pot over medium heat. When the butter starts to froth, add the onions, carrot, and salt and stir. Cover the pot and cook, stirring, until the onions are soft and creamy (without color) and the carrot is tender but firm, about 15 minutes.

Add the wine and bring to a boil. Let the wine boil until it is reduced by three-fourths, about 5 minutes. Add the pinch of chopped tarragon and 4 cups of the broth. Bring the liquid to a boil and add the peas. At this point the carrot should be cooked. Take out three-fourths of it and reserve for texture after blending. Continue cooking the peas at a simmer until they are warmed through and tender, making sure they don't lose all their green color, about 5 minutes.

Blend the mixture in batches until smooth; you will have a bright green puree. Return the puree to the large pot; add the reserved carrot pieces. Cook at a very gentle simmer for about 5 minutes, just to let the flavors develop. Season with salt to taste.

Add a generous drizzle of EVOO and several torn tarragon leaves. Then add the crème fraîche in dollops from a squeeze bottle.

In a separate pan, cook the shallots and garlic in the additional butter over medium heat. Add salt and pepper. Add the morels and slow-roast over the heat. Deglaze the pan with a ladleful of stock.

Serve the soup from the pot, with small bowls of shallots, garlic, and morels on the side.

# CHAPTER TWO

ASHA WORE SOMETHING BEAUTIFUL. SHE told me the name, but I immediately forgot. Whatever it was, I liked it, a kind of purple pantsuit with fringe around the waist and cuffs. Bridget was in black again, straight leather, suitable for nightlife in the big city but fucking silly on a brilliant, beautiful day in Solvang. Bridget was just as schoolgirl-giddy to have Asha near as I remembered. "You are too wedded to that job," I heard Bridget say. Asha shrugged.

"You know I trained to be a social worker. It's what I wanted to do, and I'm happy with my life," she said to Bridget. It was the same thing she said to me when I asked why she was so content to run a halfway house. I guess Asha was sincere in what she said to people; I admired that, and how rare it was.

At the Danish bakery that Bridget was so high on, I lingered over stale strudel while the girls stepped outside to admire bachelor's buttons and Mexican primrose growing along the road. They held hands, and I saw Bridget lean toward Asha to sneak a kiss. I hoped this Bridget knew what kind of woman she had in Asha, a human being of the first order, but that was too much to hope for. I didn't get a good feeling from Bridget. She probably thought Asha was hot and exotic, the domestic equivalent of an incendiary foreign affair without the bother of having a passport renewed. Maybe I was jealous, but I knew I was right about this Bridget and her bitch nature.

I was supposed to be put up somewhere spectacular, a woodsy resort over in the hills, with an amazing restaurant and a wonderful chef I was supposed to know. Bridget mentioned more than a half dozen times just how excited she was to take us to this paradise, but something happened to the reservation or the charge card, and plans had changed.

As we drove downhill, back to the valley, I thought we'd all be staying at Pea Soup Andersen's Inn—she mentioned that it was campy and fun—but Bridget couldn't wait to drop me off. Even so, she took the time to remind me that Monster liked prospective employees to be an hour early for interviews, to expect her to be two hours early, and with unctuous sincerity she mentioned again just how important it was to make a good impression. Oh, yes, he'd be there, he wouldn't speak and I wasn't to speak to him, but he'd be highly involved in the process.

Flow.

Monster could flow in any moment and seal the deal, but I couldn't expect that.

Of course, I'd have an in, but really, it was up to me to seize the initiative.

Dragging Asha behind her, Bridget turned her rental around and roared back to the Santa Ynez Inn. Seems Bridget had made sure the Santa Ynez Inn had one room available.

I had a bowl of very salty green soup and ate all the crackers in the cracker holder. I thought of ordering a beer; then I wanted a gin and tonic, then decided just a couple of hits off of a crack pipe would do the trick. I had another bowl of very salty green soup and found the room Bridget had reserved for me.

I turned on the television and flipped around. I watched rap videos for a while until it became painful, all of that booty shaking and with me not having got laid in almost a year. I couldn't help fantasizing being a third wheel between Asha and Bridget; maybe they would suddenly want to experiment and include me. Yeah, I couldn't sustain that fantasy; too improbable even for a hopeless optimist.

The next day Bridget was late, which meant I would probably be late. I had been up since five in the morning, so nervous about how the day would go that I went for a walk, even though a fog had rolled in, concealing Pea Soup Andersen's Inn to the point that it was difficult to know what direction to go in. I was lost almost immediately, and had to get directions from the surfer dude behind the counter at the 7-Eleven. Then I remembered I needed new razors and shaving cream.

I meandered a bit, eventually finding my way back to the hotel and my room to shave my head with the precision of an anxious man with nothing else to do.

Instinct.

It was obvious what Monster thought of himself. Look at how hard he had worked to eradicate the last vestiges of identifiable color from his life and skin.

I wouldn't let him hold that over me. Lack of melanin never held me back; actually, it was a kick, a key to acceptance that never had to be explained. Never deny it, but why let them form the question? Don't make them question their own generosity; don't make them consider the intangibles. What does it mean to hire a black man? Is it the opposite of hiring a white man, the same? Don't ask and I won't tell you.

I don't know.

I know this that Monster bolts up from night terrors, chest heaving as he rushes to the mirror to see if that bleach/chemical peel/skin brightener bled off, shed, absorbed away, or simply vanished.

Bet he lives in mortal fear of a stray BB, the living nightmare of the paralyzing threat of a nappy head.

Cool.

Even if he has a black man detector, he'll never see me coming. I don't just pass; I slip by on the strength of the fact that I can. Maybe it's self-loathing, but I never had the energy for too much of that. I am what I am: the son of two African-American parents who were light enough to pass as white if they cared to. They didn't because they were proud of who they were and embraced their African-Americanness. Monster, though, doesn't do passing. He thunders by, shouting to the world, "See me! I'm not like them, I'm you!"

He hides in plain sight, and I guess I do too. Race explains nothing about his insanity, or my blundering into acceptance and not wanting to rock the boat. Probably, in that sense, we're brothers under the skin.

Bridget showed two hours late, a woman in desperate need of a toilet but without a bit of an apology other than a curt "Monster rescheduled" before she hauled ass to the bathroom.

"Where's Asha?" I asked after she returned. I needed to see a friendly face, and Bridget wasn't it.

"Sleeping in. She needs it," Bridget said, with a hint of a leer, and I disliked her even more. It still ain't polite to hit it and strut. As much as I admired and liked Asha, I couldn't understand her taste in women.

Bridget sped to the 101 and headed east, back toward Santa Barbara. Another stunningly beautiful day; from the freeway I could see the Pacific lurking behind the hammock of hills, and when we started to climb and banked west, I saw surfers, black stick figures on breaking waves.

Then Bridget turned east and we headed into the Santa Ynez valley.

At an access road Bridget drove for another twenty minutes or so, until an official-looking craftsman bungalow came into view. Near the bungalow was an impressive gate, maybe ten feet high, blocking a well-maintained road.

A man in a gray uniform with a cap like that of a highway patrolman from the forties leaned into the window and thrust a clipboard into my hands. On the clipboard was a document that went on for four pages. I hadn't got through the first page before Bridget tapped me on the shoulder.

"It's a release. You can't interview without signing it."

"Give me a minute. I like to read before I sign."

She sighed and watched with narrowed eyes as I hastily flipped through the document.

"Done? Good. Now, sign."

I signed and handed the clipboard back to the security guard.

Bridget burned rubber on the way out, as though she had to make up lost time, but I thought we were early. About a mile later she stopped at another bungalow, just as gray and official-looking as the last one, but with two very busy men sorting through packages stacked in the driveway. Bridget waved to them and headed inside and pointed to an oversize leather chair by a window. I sat down as she flipped through more paperwork. The interior of the bungalow resembled the layout of a nicely appointed law office. I remembered wanting to buy those heavy brass lamps with the handblown leaded glass for the restaurant, but gave up when I couldn't get a reasonable price.

"Wait here. The head of Security will be by in a few minutes to begin the interview. Then, afterward, maybe Monster will be ready to ask you a few questions."

I leaned back in my chair, crossed my legs, and tried to look calm as I waited for my life to resume.

A door opened. A tall man entered, dressed in the uniform that all these guys sported, as though they could change your oil, carry your luggage, or arrest you. All of them were trim, tall, and white; did Monster hire every washed-out Mormon FBI agent he could find?

Bridget handed him a ream of paper, and he walked over to me with his hand out and paused, squinting as though he recognized me and he wasn't happy about it.

"Mr. Gibson, my name is Timothy Steele. I run Security here at the Lair. I wonder if you could clarify a few things."

"Sure, I'll do my best."

"You were arrested for attempting to buy a controlled substance. Is that correct?"

"Yes."

"What was the controlled substance?"

"Heroin, to smoke. Usually it was cocaine, but the time I was arrested it was heroin."

He paused for a moment and thumbed through the documentation on the clipboard, then returned his unblinking attention to me.

"You don't have any prior arrests?"

"Nope. I've lived a pretty straight life, other than my recent drug experience. I've received the best treatment and diversion therapy possible, and I've been clean for a year."

"That's good to hear, but you should know that we do an ongoing security check on all employees. If at some point we discover that you concealed any aspect of your personal history, no matter the relevance, you will be terminated immediately."

I paused for a moment, wanting very much to tell him to fuck himself, that I didn't need this fucking job. However, I did need it. I needed to get back to a life that wasn't embarrassing. Oh, yeah, I needed this job in the worst way.

I allowed myself hope, a threadbare hope I kept in a sock drawer in the hidden closet in the back room of my confidence, the sad little hope that I could resurrect my career, that I wouldn't fuck up, that somehow, through some voodoo, I could make Elena want me again, that I wouldn't make my life a slow suicide, that I'd finally shake that fear that I was out to do myself in, that I couldn't trust myself.

I couldn't afford to tell anybody to fuck off, except for maybe myself.

"I told you everything, except for when I got drunk as an undergraduate and wore this coed's panties home on my head. I guess that could be considered a crime."

Mr. Security gave me a look, a look of disdain, mild disgust. Then, like the sun breaking through the clouds, he smiled.

"I don't think I'll need to make note of that."

That seemed to lighten the ultraserious moment.

"Good," I said, and stood to leave.

"One more thing," he said.

He handed me a paper bag. I looked inside and saw a plastic cup with a lid.

"We need a urine sample. If you're offered the job, you'll be subject to regular random drug tests."

My pride sloughed off like a skin I didn't need. I dutifully took the paper bag and went into the restroom.

I was in luck. Someone had pinned the sports page above the urinal; the Giants were on a winning streak. Quite a few of the workers at the Lair must have to submit to this weekly ritual. I handed the warm container to Security and saw Bridget waving at me.

"Yes, he just came in. Do you want me to put him on?"

She gestured for me to sit down, her eyes flaring as though she'd toss a book at my head if I delayed for a second.

"Use the speakerphone."

I nodded, confused as to who I was talking to and why.

"Hello?"

I heard breathing, kind of raspy. I grinned at how silly this felt.

"This is Monster." His voice didn't have that ethereal quality I'd heard in those interviews on VH1. He sounded grounded, even a little hard.

"It's an honor to talk with you," I said.

"What's your name again?"

"William Gibson."

"Right, you're the cat who owned the restaurant in New York. You lost it because of drugs."

"Yeah, that's about it."

"It would be cool if we could hire you."

"I would like that very much," I said, wondering what would stop him if he wanted to hire me.

"But I need to ask you a question and you need to answer me honestly. Can you do that?"

"Yes, I can do that."

"Good."

I waited for him to ask the question, but he went back to that raspy breathing, as though he had a problem with his sinuses.

"Doyouthinkyoucanplayme?"

He blurted it out so fast, at first I couldn't make out what he said.

"Could you repeat that?"

"Ha!" he said, with a snort. Then he spelled it out for me. "Do . . . you . . . think . . . you . . . can . . . play . . . me?"

"What?"

"You know what I'm saying."

"I'm not sure what you mean."

Monster paused as though he was ready to drop the bomb on me.

"You gonna play me? Are you gonna play me?"

"I pride myself on my professionalism. I don't take it lightly."

"I'm not talking about that."

I wanted to ask what was he talking about, but I figured that wouldn't get me hired.

"I'm a very loyal employee. That's how I've always been. It's second nature to me."

"It's more than loyalty."

"I'm not sure I understand what you're saying."

"Then that means you're not down. I only hire down cats."

I was beyond confused.

"I'll ask you once more. Are you gonna play me?"

"I don't intend to play you."

Another pause and more raspy breathing.

"I'm supposed to believe you? I think you're lying. Tell me this, are you experienced?"

"What, in a Jimi Hendrix way?"

"Yeah, exactly. That's exactly what I'm saying. You've got to be down for me."

My stomach sank. If he thought I was going to be getting loaded with him after dinner, that wasn't where my head was at. "I understand!" I said.

"Understand what?"

"What you said about being down."

"Being down? What did I say about that?"

Now, my breathing was all raspy. Was he high? He had to be high; only people who were fucked up out of their minds but who thought they were under control talked like that.

"Long as you down for me it's all true. You know what I'm saying," he said, excitedly.

"Yeah," I said, nodding, even though I knew he couldn't see me unless he had a hidden camera. That I wouldn't put past him.

"Are you gonna poison me?" he blurted, surprising the hell out of me. Of all the crazy-assed things I've been asked in my life, this surprised me into stupid silence.

"I've never poisoned anyone," I said, with conviction.

More raspy breathing.

"You're not gonna put anything sick into my food?"

"Sick?"

"Are you going to poison me?"

"I can't say you'll love everything I'll cook, but I can guarantee I'll never poison you."

"Ha, you funny. I'll get back to you."

The speakerphone went silent.

Bridget looked at me with suspicion.

"Did you have any idea what you were saying?"

I nodded without conviction.

"Monster likes people to be straight with him."

"I was being straight. What, I didn't sound straight?"

Bridget snorted.

"I don't think you knew what you were saying. You were willing to say anything to get him to hire you."

I never did like this Bridget, and she didn't like me. If it weren't for Asha, I'm sure she wouldn't have had anything to do with me. I didn't have a problem with that except for the fact that I did need this job.

"I don't see what the problem is. We seem to have hit it off."

"First of all, that wasn't Monster."

"Huh? Who was it?"

"Monster's assistant."

"Assistant? He sounds like a thug high on something."

"Well, he is a thug. He calls himself Thug. That's his name as far as you're concerned."

I felt tricked. It wasn't right and Bridget needed to know how I felt.

"Bridget, you know I need this job, but obviously you don't feel good about me applying for it. Am I wasting my time?"

Bridget looked surprised, as if I had just come out of left field with that. She wouldn't look me in the eye.

"Is it Asha? You promised her something and now you don't want to deliver?"

Bridget ran her hands through her hair, still avoiding my eyes.

"You might want this job, I know you need it, but once you get out there, it's different. I'm always looking for employees. It's a fucking strain. The lawyers, God, I talk to so many lawyers."

"That's big of you, trying to spare me some grief."

Finally, our eyes met. She looked like a woman who'd had enough.

"I've got my share of problems. I'll admit that. You're right. Asha really wants this for you."

"You don't think I'm capable?"

She shook her head.

"It's not that at all. I don't want to have to answer to Asha when it's over."

"What do you mean 'when it's over'? What do you have to answer for?"

"I might be a little jealous about how much she likes you, but it's not all jealousy. I just don't want her blaming me when everything goes to hell."

I stood up to leave. I was through with this shit.

"I finished that diversion program with no problems. You know that."

"Oh, this isn't about you. It's about Monster, and it's about why I want to quit this job. I don't want to be responsible for the shit that happens."

"Quit this job? I don't get you at all! You bring me in, then decide I'm not right for the position, and then you tell me you're gonna quit."

"Don't get so pissed off. If I get the call that he wants to offer you the job, I'm not going to disagree. I'm not that kind of bitch. I'm just being up front. You need to know what you're getting into."

"What are you talking about? What am I getting into?"

"You'll see. You'll have to see how this place works. You'll know soon enough if you've got the stomach for it."

The phone rang and she snatched it up with a crisp "Bridget here."

I walked outside before hearing the verdict: Would I live or die? Was I hired, or was I flying back to the halfway house to finish probation? At that moment I just wanted to feel the sun on my skin, whatever the hell happened.

## GRILLED CHEESE SANDWICHES WITH ROASTED SWEET POTATO

SERVES 4

2 sweet potatoes
Extra-virgin olive oil (EVOO), as needed for brushing
Salt and freshly ground black pepper
4 tablespoons unsalted butter
3 cipolline onions, peeled and julienned
3 teaspoons brown sugar
2 tablespoons balsamic vinegar
¼ pound Brie, chilled
¼ pound fontina
8 slices potato bread
Whole-grain mustard

Peel the sweet potatoes, slice into 2-inch rounds, brush with EVOO, and sprinkle with salt and pepper. Bake in a 375°F oven until fork-tender, about 15 minutes. Set aside.

Heat 2 tablespoons butter in a 12-inch heavy nonstick skillet over moderately high heat. When the butter is foamy, add the onions, salt, ½ teaspoon black pepper, sugar, and vinegar and cook until the onions are caramelized, about 8 minutes. Set aside and let cool to room temperature.

Remove and discard the cheese rinds. Mix the cheeses and divide the mixture among 4 slices of the potato bread, using about ¼ cup per slice. Layer the sweet potato rounds on top of the cheese. Spread the remaining 4 slices of bread with the mustard and the onion mixture and place (mustard side down) on top of each sandwich.

Heat 1 tablespoon butter in a clean skillet over moderate heat until it starts to foam. Then cook 2 sandwiches, without turning them over, until the undersides are golden brown, about 3 minutes. Transfer the sandwiches to a cutting board. Heat 1 tablespoon butter in the skillet until foaming starts, then return the sandwiches to the skillet, browned sides up, and cook 3 minutes more. Transfer them back to the cutting board when cooked. Repeat with the remaining 2 sandwiches.

Trim off the crusts and cut each sandwich into fourths.

Optional: Top each piece with a drop of truffle oil.

# CHAPTER THREE

SOMETIMES I THINK I HEAR HIM CALLING, a sibilant whisper from a satin-lined oak coffin hidden below the subbasement in a tomb so cold he'd be able to see his rancid breath if he actually had breath. "Living Food, that's what I'm feeling," he says.

Because he's feeling it, I'm feeling it, and that's why I'm drinking that Santa Ynez Sauvignon Blanc. I'm liking it more than I should.

Backsliding. No more of this drinking after work, getting silly, having flights of fancy that do me no good. I've still got to deal with Living Food, no matter how silly it is to consider cooking without fire an earthshaking invention. Really, you'd think most reasonable people would agree that cooking is a good thing, a good invention, and we should feel good about it. Maybe Monster remembered something about predigestion in high school biology and it confused and disgusted him. Probably, though, it's the influence of a gastronomic guru who put him on the road to bliss through the chewing of fresh ginger. Who am I to stand in the way of his path to enlightenment?

Monster is a freak, a freakish freak, but he's not a creature-feature villain, no matter how wine might insinuate that. No.

He's a self-invented American, freakishly fascinating in his attempt at reinvention, and because of it, his self-invention, his desire to live like something out of a cautionary tale of how outrageously wrong famous people go, doesn't necessarily make him unique, just as unique as crazy wealth and an addiction to television can make him. I bet as a kid he rushed home to watch *Dark Shadows* with a chaser of *The Brady Bunch*, which explains some of it—the blond children running around like chickens shooed about by giddy parents. Really, it's not Monster or the kids I wonder about; it's the parents. What must they be like? What do they want for themselves, for their children?

I'm sure they have lawyers on speed dial, ready and waiting for something actionable. Maybe that's Monster's real value, pulling back the curtain on the banality of human perversity—give somebody like him enough money and power and see what gets revealed.

He's fucking crazy, but it's okay.

Everyone here knows it. It's common knowledge, living

up here on the mountain. When will the townspeople realize what's up and break out the torches and pitchforks and march on Monster's Lair? Isn't it inevitable?

I have another glass of wine and try to return my attention to the task at hand: planning Monster's meals for the week. I figured when I first saw him that the last thing he would be concerned about is eating, figuring him as a man who lived on meth and Twinkies and maybe Diet Coke, because these folks bathe themselves in Diet Coke. For a man over six feet, he must weigh a hundred twenty pounds, and that's if he hasn't evacuated his bowels. Considering what he wants to eat, he'd be better served by hiring a botanist than a personal chef. "Living Food" isn't something a cook makes. No, give a kid mud, wheat, and water and whatever and let him go at it.

But I'm a professional; if that's what Monster is into this week, I'll give it to him straight, with a sprig of fresh rosemary on that sunbaked gluten-free ravioli.

*Breakfast*

Sun-roasted oatmeal with coconut milk and raisins

*Snack*

Cracked barley porridge with fresh strawberries

*Lunch*

Vegan sunbaked pizza with three kinds of tomato
and Mexican salt from Oaxaca

*Snack*

Fresh greens in a lemon sauce

*Dinner*

Veggie sushi

*Snack*

Unsweetened cider

AT THE CENTER OF MONSTER'S LAIR was a stone mansion that resembled a castle, but it had far too many windows. A plumber, there for a few days to work on a secret new project that required an earthmover, mentioned an old project as I made him a sandwich. He whispered that he suspected Monster saved his piss, had some sort of trough in the master bedroom that drained into a cistern.

"Howard Hughes complex."

The plumber laughed and asked for another sandwich.

"My ex-wife was into that," he said between bites of his sandwich. "Back in the eighties in Santa Barbara people did a lot of weird shit. I think it was all that cocaine going around."

I offered him lemonade, and he revealed more intriguing information.

"I thought it was the biggest pool we've ever dug. It was

in the shape of an O, and it ran all around the mansion. The contractor said it was the first fucking moat he had ever built. A month after we first filled it with water, a truck arrived, tipped backward, and toothy fish tumbled out," the plumber said with a shrug.

"I guess he's got security concerns."

Monster had a moat, and I know we were all expected to be overwhelmed and maybe intimidated; why would you pay for a moat if not to impress the world with it? Impressed or not, you get over that sort of thing pretty quickly, though it was more irritating than impressive to cross a moat to go to the mansion kitchen, having to wait for Security to check their stupid clipboard before lowering the drawbridge. I guess they had to do that, though I had been running the kitchen for months. I'd heard the rumors that the stalker was still at it, trying to find a way into Monster's Lair.

Yeah, I suppose there was some truth to it, just as I suspected there was some truth to the rumor I made up that Monster has a dungeon with chains hanging from the walls, an iron maiden, and all the other tools of the trade. Say that to a hungry plumber and you know that story will accelerate until it achieves enough escape velocity to take off and maybe make the pages of the *National Enquirer* or Fox News. What else are you gonna do if rumors are thick as pea soup around you but be a rumormonger?

THE RED FLAG STOOD AT ATTENTION on the old-fashioned mailbox in front of my bungalow. Can't say I didn't feel mild dread. I guess it was better than having to meet with whoever it was who ran the day-to-day business of Monster's Lair. I don't know why disembodied directives make me so nervous. I guess it's better than having someone disagreeable in my face, giving me shit, but the notes were always in an envelope and on expensive paper and handwritten, and they got to the point with few words. Turns out I had good reason to be afraid; this letter was on the subject of a party for Monster's birthday involving two hundred very important guests who would be expecting to enjoy a meal of the healthiest and most invigorating food direct from my kitchen.

I imagined myself going slowly nuts trying to develop a menu based on uncooked vegetables, without sugar, milk, butter, cheese, meat, just about everything. Then and there I was of the mind to quit, go back to the halfway house and return to long hours of labor in the kitchen. I had no choice but to educate myself in this food and the idea behind it. Research would save me.

I looked up everything I could on the subject and, after hours of reading, decided what these super-vegans wanted was a good, quick, cleansing fast. They wanted the discipline of monks, denying themselves, mortifying the flesh, forgoing the temptations of this life.

Taste equals illusion.

They wanted something real, realer than real, blander than bland, and, consequently, healthy. I wondered what Monster wanted. Did he want to achieve higher consciousness? It had to be that because he certainly couldn't want to lose weight unless he wanted to be a hunger artist and fade away into a disembodied voice, rocking to broad daylight. I decided to make mixed salad with lots of olives. Thank God for the wonderful local olives.

**Notes on dinner menu:** *Monster will not eat peanuts or olives, and he doesn't care for tomatoes or lemons or lemon juice.*

Fuck the local olives, they weren't that good anyway.

JUST A DAY BEFORE Monster's birthday party an incredibly expensive events catering company arrived in convoys of semis that polluted the air so thoroughly with dust and diesel that I thought the festivities would be disastrous. But like clockwork they assembled a Disneyfied bedouin camp with elegant tents arranged along the extensive grounds outside of the Lair proper. My job was to oversee the caterers, but there was no need; the hospitality crew, the food and liquor, the entertainment were all top flight, seemingly superhuman, and as far as I could see weren't doing speed or coke. My menu wasn't discarded; worse, it had been improved on. I milled around pretending to be busy while they slaved to make everything work seamlessly with skill and determined purpose.

How much did these people get paid? I thought as I tried to stay out of the way and tried not to look totally useless. Finally I gave in and watched the stars arrive—the Saudi royalty, and the Eurotrash, and the handsome quarterback who had a triumphant Super Bowl two years ago, but more recent play had resulted in his being traded to the dregs of the league where he became ensnared in a scandal involving an Instagram indiscretion. The woman he had with him, a blonde who had to be at least five foot seven but still wore six-inch heels, stood nearly at his height but rail thin with such a ridiculous purchased rack that she looked as though she might pitch over at any moment. Always, these couples were the most likely to be the unhappiest diners at my restaurant. The men were always uninterested in the women and the women either hung on to the men as if they might get away or were like this one, trying to get as much juice out of a temporary situation as possible. She stood at the bar and immediately began throwing back martinis and when sufficiently sauced tottered over, with the grim-faced quarterback lagging behind, to the burning-hot new singer with the dangling earrings and Yakuza-like tattoos who had the habit of beating up his boyfriends in public. The tattooed singer–bad boy ignored them and rushed away to witness the arrival of the Jesus, Buddha, and Gandhi of hip-hop with his cruel empress wife whose assistants elbowed clear a space near the pool and maneuvered them to where their best angles were the only angles available. They posed like glamorous store mannequins for the official paparazzi to immortalize them, but they were lost in the typhoon of Monster's arrival. Not just wearing a tight black suit, he wore the blackness of the abyss, a glittering light-eating material of a suit. The power couple of the moment tried to approach Monster as equals, joking and back slapping, with the assembled luminaries reduced to witnesses to the spectacle of their celestial brilliance, but Monster's aspect was rising; he wasn't just a star, he was transcendent.

I wanted to hit up tattooed singer–bad boy to share some of the cocaine he was snorting openly, but I decided against it, thinking that detached amusement was the way to go. The JBG of hip-hop and his empress gestured for one of their assistants to hand Monster a box that shook as though something was alive inside of it. Monster's assistant took the box away and I hoped that whatever was in there didn't need to breathe much. Monster swept them both up in his thin arms and kissed them like long-lost children. Everyone was delighted.

I thought I saw David Bowie—he came to the opening of my restaurant years ago and had many kind words—but it wasn't him, probably just a rail-thin white man appropriating his image. My energy started to flag as I watched the luminaries arrive and frolic, as if frolicking was texting and shaping photos as they halfheartedly chatted. A gong rang, loud and sharp, and Monster suddenly was on a stage, illuminated in such harsh white light that it was almost impossible to look at him. A tsunami of techno dub enveloped us in bone-rattling bass and Monster exploded in twirling movement faster than I thought possible. His limbs multiplied Kali-like, writhing, elongating, pulsating in the firing of syncopated strobe lights. The black that he wore made his white translucent skin more ghostly and ethereal, even angelic. My hard-fought detachment bled away and my heart pounded, giddy with the sheer excitement of being in his presence; the special effects that embodied his every move were proof that he was the end-all, the be-all, and I was lucky to be in his presence, to serve him. The performance didn't last long, like the jolt of the first hit off of a crack pipe after hard-earned sobriety.

"Thank you so very much for coming and sharing my birthday!" Monster said, his voice like ice shards. Then from his hands came smoke, and it all seemed magical, more magical than I could have believed, and the smoke snaking from his hands began to sparkle like stars in a black Texas night so subtly that if you weren't concentrating you'd miss it. Soon the entire vastness of the bedouin tent was filled with the twinkling smoke that smelled slightly of jasmine. It was delightful. Another gong rang and the smoke and Monster disappeared. Bright lights broke the spell and the catering crew got to serving my modified vegan menu. I felt happy and content as I watched the clockwork precision of the servers, and the food even seemed tempting if I'd had any appetite.

Happy. I was fucking happy . . . I can't be happy, I thought, then it occurred to me that my happiness corresponded with the smoke, and as the smoke dissipated so did my unearned happiness. The gathering began to break up almost before the mountainous vegan birthday cake was served. Monster never returned; instead tattooed singer–bad boy led the luminaries in a spirited happy birthday sing-along to a three-dimensional projection of Monster standing like a colossus above Monster's Lair, waving good-bye. Oh, yes, if only I were blunted . . . maybe then I could laugh.

THE MANSION HAD INNER GROUNDS; the kitchen faced the vegetable garden, and beyond the vegetable garden was the most elaborate playland I had ever seen. It was as if the carnival had come to town. Security made sure I didn't get too close to the carousel and its intricately carved unicorns and flying horses, or the incongruous Ferris wheel standing tall among the oaks and eucalyptus, or the miniature train at rest, large enough to transport a dozen kids around the grounds under the elms and oaks and around the acres and acres of Monster's Lair. But nothing surprised me more than the Middle-earth model/diorama near the eastern wall of the playground. Mount Doom stood five feet high with some kind of volcano action churning and frothing from within. Everything from the Shire to Gondor was represented, and everywhere were lifelike figures occupying the land, all the Orcs, Elves, and Hobbits you could expect to see in the Middle-earth of Monster's imagination.

I have to admit that I wanted to get a closer look, to examine Gandalf and the rest of them, but the moment I crossed the invisible line, Security appeared to shoo me away with a curt "This isn't for the public."

I wanted to say that I wasn't the public, that I needed some diversion from doing the nothing I had been doing since I was hired.

Monster was out of the country, on tour, and his traveling chef went with him, so my cooking for him was up until this point mostly theoretical. As his personal chef who stayed home at the Lair, I was supposed to "get the lay of the land" while he was gone. To this day I wonder why that expression meant so much to Monster. It was used repeatedly in the directives I received in the tastefully weathered mailbox in front of my bungalow. I quickly came to hate the constant memos about the importance of keeping silent about life at the Lair because that's the "lay of the land." Did that phrase convey the seriousness and weight that Monster wanted but couldn't secure because, well, he was a freak?

I didn't have a damn thing to do but tend the herb garden that was essential to Living Food cuisine and prepare menus and wonder what I had got myself into, being paid decently for nothing more than waking up and wondering about my ability to make life decisions; should I do push-ups, have scrambled eggs for breakfast, call Elena and beg forgiveness, or sit on the toilet for an hour, reading culinary magazines? I hated wasting time as much as I hated having none of it back when I had the restaurant, none of it for myself when I had a life. This half life gave me time enough to drown in memories of Elena from when I had a full life that wasn't enough for me, though it was everything I could ever want or need. I'd see her lying twisted in white sheets in the morning, making eggs for breakfast with her short nightgown on, her hair messy about her head, her face still swollen from sleep like a child. I'd see her reaching for my hand as we walked through Central Park, searching for a breeze on a hot day. Maybe most men aren't monogamous, and one woman is interchangeable with another, but that's not me. I'm like a fucking wolf or swan. I wanted Elena. The only other loves I had were work and coke, equal addictions; wanting Elena was everlasting. She defined my life and I killed my life, but my love for her wouldn't die. I could taste her lips against mine and spin into the history of our relationship, the first time I thrust inside of her, the first time I heard her gasp as she came. All that mattered to me . . . gone, and what was left was the bitter taste of Living Food.

It was a little unnerving how quiet the grounds of the Lair were; the birds sang muted songs, and I never heard crickets or bees.

Unnaturally silent.

I had far too much time to mull over everything, until mulling became so unappealingly tedious that I couldn't mull if I wanted to.

Turned down the volume and slipped into a state of stultifying boredom. I never suspected spending the foreseeable future in beautiful seclusion would drive me fucking nuts. Maybe I should have had an idea that this wasn't a life for me. Bridget might be a bitch, but she was right about this soul-poisoning Lair; it made you want to drown in a river of fine Santa Ynez wine.

I WOKE UP DREAMING of Elena again, remembering cyberstalking her back when I could use the computer at the halfway house. I prowled through her Facebook page, seeing the man she was with, a buffoonish, long-haired idiot some years younger than me, with a ridiculous shit-eating grin. My heart ached as I saw them together, arm in arm, a fucking couple. Seeing the photo of her making gumbo, in the kitchen I used to cook in, probably using my Sriracha sauce, photo shot by *him*. I imagined pounding him into the ground, repeatedly, endlessly. I couldn't hate her, but I certainly could hate him. I researched this loser and discovered he was some sort of homeopath, a healer, which made me hate him even more. I wanted my wife, my life back. I wanted to forget all of it. Get a do-over, that's all I wanted. But what I got were lucid dreams of holding the woman I loved and left for a crack pipe.

ON THE BACK STEP of the kitchen, with a big metal bowl between my legs, I was absentmindedly shelling peas while listening to *Rastaman Vibration*, fantasizing that I was trapped in a beautiful Babylon, when I saw her by the pineapple sage, sniffing at red blossoms, shooing away bees: a very pregnant blonde who looked almost comic, that thin with such a belly! I waved to her and she glanced up. She looked alarmed and hurried to the private entrance of the mansion that the hired help could not, under any circumstances, use. As soon as she disappeared a powerfully built black man appeared. He wore baggy linen pants and a white shirt so tight that if he flexed his muscles it would burst. He turned and looked at me; his face expressed nothing.

But I got it, another indication of this "lay of the land" warning: Don't even look in the direction of Monster's wife.

Or you might have a brother man come calling.

I WANTED TO TELL MANNY the groundskeeper what had happened, but I didn't know if I could trust him, or anyone at Monster's Lair.

Once or twice a week Manny came by the kitchen for fruit juice. I enjoyed his visits, and the distraction from the monotony of doing very little. He watched happily as I cut watermelon and put it into the processor with sugar and a little lemon.

I served it to him in a frosted glass, and he seemed to be genuinely impressed.

"It's good," he said, "almost like what you would get in Mexico."

I had returned to chopping carrots when I saw him glance at me.

"You like working here?" he asked.

I shrugged. "I can't say I like it, but I'm almost used to it. This place . . . I don't know what to say about this place. It's so quiet; sometimes I go a whole day and not say a word to anyone. I'm not sure why Monster needs a personal chef. He hardly spends any time here. Hear he's in Poland trying to get an amusement park built. There's really nothing much for me to do. Sometimes I get stir-crazy with hardly anyone to talk to. It's like I'm serving a prison sentence in solitary confinement."

Manny nodded.

"Yes. They paid for us to come to work, but there isn't

much work. But for me it's good. I've worked hard all my life and now I get paid well to not work too hard. The drive home, it's hard, the drive to Lompoc, but I don't mind. I don't like to stay here nights. My wife doesn't like to be alone, so I only stay when the weather is bad and I don't trust the road," Manny said, and looked nervous for a second and then continued in a barely audible voice, "I try not to stay here after dark."

"Why?"

Manny didn't answer and refused to meet my eyes.

"But as long as you're not here at night, you're okay with the job?"

"I make good money. I'm able to put aside money for retiring. I've already had a home built in Baja for when I retire. I can't complain about this job. It's been good to me."

"You work over there in the forbidden courtyard?"

"Forbidden courtyard, that's what you call it?"

"Yeah, it's a joke to myself. What goes on over there, what do you see?"

Manny smiled broadly. "You signed that paper. We're not supposed to talk about what we see."

"But I've yet to actually see anything. Other than a couple of quick stops, Monster has been gone for most of the time I've worked here."

"Good for you. It's nice when he's not here. When he is, Security is too *bravo*. You don't need these to work here," Manny said, pointing to his eyes, then to his ears.

"Ears either," I said.

We laughed, and then I stared at him for a minute, hoping that maybe he'd let something slip.

"Those young boys are everywhere. They uproot plantings and break things, but you can't talk to them. No, Security won't let you stop them from doing a thing. He wants them to do what they do, and make the mess they make."

"Me, I don't see much. I stay in the kitchen. I've never seen Monster anywhere near the kitchen. Security comes for his meals and that's that. They give me a list of things for the week he might be interested in, and I try to figure out how to make it palatable."

"What does he eat?"

I hesitated for a minute. Those confidentiality agreements were very explicit.

"Me, I don't see much, either."

"Oh, come on. Tell me. He eats bugs and rats and drinks blood?"

"He might, but I'm not saying."

"Amigo, you can tell me, and this tale will stay in this kitchen."

"You tell me something about the woman, and I'll tell you something about what Monster eats."

"*Sí*. That's fair," Manny said with a solemn nod.

"Most of the time, I don't make him anything. I get notes about his ideas about food theory, but I hardly cook anything for him. Once, when he was back from tour, he asked for eggs and toast for breakfast. He wanted the eggs to be poached, just so, in white wine from the Santa Ynez Valley, and he has to have toast baked fresh each morning from organic whole grain flour from France. He's obsessed with genetically modified food and doesn't trust American flour. He never touched the eggs or the toast. He ate the butter and jam, mixes it together and spoons it out of the jar. Far as I know that's pretty much what he lives off, and that's why he looks like shit on a stick, ghastly pale. Mostly I cook for his wife. I suspect it's kind of an experiment; I don't know this for a fact, but I suspect he feeds her what he thinks would be the best and healthiest, but for himself he goes to McDonald's for Big Macs."

"Oh," Manny said, dejectedly, as though he had counted on confirmation that Monster snacked on raw monkey brains.

"Okay, about the woman."

Manny looked about the room as though we were being spied on.

"She can't talk."

"What do you mean she can't talk?"

"She is . . . How do you call it in English? You know, those people who can't talk. Deaf?"

"No, deaf is when you can't hear. You mean she's a mute?"

"Does that mean she can't talk?"

"Yes, exactly."

"She can't say a thing. Once she got lost on the grounds,

not really lost, but Security was busy with Monster and the kids. They didn't see her take the hillside path, the one that washed out, and she fell, hurt her ankle."

"What happened?"

"She cried, but no words. I ran down the hillside from where I had been pruning trees. I asked whether she was hurt in Spanish and English, and she started with her hands and fingers, and I got nervous and called Security. I didn't know this lady, but from the way Security acted she had to be somebody important. One of them used his hands the way she did, and they helped her into one of their golf carts and took her away."

"I saw her yesterday. I didn't say a word, but I made eye contact with her and she walked away. Then this muscle-bound black guy comes out of nowhere and does his best to stare me down."

Manny nodded. "So you met Mr. Thug?"

"Mr. Thug? Is that Monster's assistant?"

"Yes, that's him."

"I don't call that meeting someone. I mean all he did was stare at me, like he wanted to beat the shit out of me."

Manny shrugged. "You need to keep away from Mr. Thug. He's trouble."

"Trouble? I wasn't trying to make conversation with him. I wave to Mrs. Monster, she leaves, and he comes over and mad-dogs me."

"Mad-dogs you? Yeah, that's a good description of Mr. Thug. That's why you should stay far from him."

Manny finished the juice and nodded his thanks and headed out from the shelter of the kitchen into the bright and harsh afternoon sun.

The story seemed straight enough, and though I didn't know Manny well, I had no reason to doubt him. I wasn't surprised that Monster would be interested in a woman, though I assumed he was gay. Being filthy rich made anything possible, though. I was surprised he'd be interested in a mute. I figured him for the kind of star who would require a perfect trophy wife so he could have perfect trophy children and they all could live in his weird little kingdom of monsters. Maybe I had to reconsider him; he wasn't a totally lunatic superstar, seeking perfection in everything in the blind hope that perfection would rub off on him.

## SPICED BHINDI AND EGGPLANT

SERVES 4

4 ounces bhindi (okra)
3 to 4 cloves garlic
Extra-virgin olive oil (EVOO)
3 shallots, peeled and diced
½ teaspoon cumin seeds
4 ounces mini eggplant, chopped
1 large heirloom tomato, finely chopped
¼ teaspoon turmeric
Salt
½ teaspoon smoked paprika
¼ teaspoon garam masala
½ teaspoon coriander
¼ teaspoon fresh Thai chili, minced
1 tablespoon cilantro, finely chopped
Juice of 2 limes (freshly squeezed)

A few hours before cooking, wash and drain the bhindi; remove and discard the heads and tails; and slice the okra into ⅓-inch rounds. Also beforehand, slow-fry the garlic in EVOO. Remove and mash the garlic, reserving the EVOO.

When cooking begins, warm the reserved garlic oil in a nonstick pan or wok over medium heat and sauté the shallots. Add the cumin seeds and when they begin to crackle, add the garlic; sauté for 30 seconds.

Add the bhindi and eggplant and mix well. Cook on medium heat, stirring often, until the eggplant and bhindi get color, about 7 minutes. Add the tomato, turmeric, and salt; cook until the tomato is tender, about 2 minutes. Add the paprika, garam masala, coriander, and Thai chili and mix well. Cook for about 1 minute over medium heat. Toss in the cilantro. Add the lime juice.

Optional: Garnish with micro cilantro.

# CHAPTER FOUR

AFTER BREAKFAST I USUALLY TENDED THE herb garden. Mornings were pleasant as I warmed in the sun, smelling rosemary and thyme in the air, on my fingers. Mornings made Monster's Lair seem a good place to work and my life sensible, though there're only so many times you can rearrange a kitchen, sharpen cutlery, clean and reclean surfaces so as to make them antiseptic. Eventually, I had a dozen kinds of yeast, six kinds of salt, more kinds of vinegar than I would ever need. I made sure to stock up on all the trace elements that the chemistry of Living Food required: talc of mustard seed, pregnant nut extract, dried blackberry juice.

Though I told myself I would not mull, it wasn't humanly possible to escape doing so. I came to the conclusion that the real reason for my job was to be a placeholder and keep the kitchen occupied because Monster could afford me, and since he had the money, he had to have a chef. And if that chef, even with an arrest record, once was somebody, he needed me on his payroll.

I was an ornament on the Christmas tree of his success.

Monster became more a presence than a real human employer. Some nights I'd see lights flash by as a caravan of limos made their way onto the grounds. I thought then I'd get the call to be ready to serve Monster, but it didn't come. Maybe he brought home takeout or stopped at the Carrows off the 101, but I doubted that.

I worked for a ghost, an invisible man.

But in the mornings unease about a ghostly employer felt silly.

At night it was a different story. When it's dark and cold and the fire dies down in the hearth, yeah, imagining what went on in that mansion wasn't pleasant at all.

I heard a gate open and turned from tending the herb garden to see Monster's wife, now heavily pregnant, meandering in the rose garden. Her nurse, a big-haired white woman, hung back, fumbling with a magazine on a bench beneath a tree. Monster's wife slowly cut roses, smelled each one, and dropped them into a wicker basket. Hand on her back, she waddled from plant to plant, taking a stem or two. She had to be maybe eight and a half months' pregnant, and she looked striking, with her blond hair glinting gold in the gray, moist morning air. She stopped the trimming of roses and stared at me.

I stared back. I wasn't supposed to, not after that situation with Thug. I didn't want that fool causing me grief.

It was all very clear to me now: Don't address Monster's wife; don't talk to the children.

Mind your own damn business.

She held a white rose to her nose and sniffed and sneezed.

I laughed, and she looked at me with narrowed eyes.

"Sorry," I said with a shrug.

Frowning, she turned toward the mansion and waddled away.

My stomach sank. I imagined her using sign language to convey just what a pig I had been.

Thug would return with Security and have me hauled off to the dungeon. No, they'd just fire me and I'd be back on a plane, flying to New Jersey to return to the halfway house.

I was so lost in thought that I pretty much denuded a rosemary shrub and didn't see Monster's wife return with paper and pen.

She flung open the wrought iron gate separating the staff from the inner courtyard. She made her way to me, scribbling ferociously.

I waited, wondering what she had written, what kind of trouble she was about to inflict on me. She thrust the paper into my hands.

She had written in a flowing hand, *You were laughing at me!*

"No," I said.

She shook her head and pointed to the paper and handed me the pen.

I wrote quickly.

*I wasn't laughing at you. I just thought you looked beautiful. Mothers-to-be are beautiful.*

She seemed to hiccup, but then I realized it was a giggle.

I scribbled, *When are you due?*

She took the paper from me.

*Three weeks.*

*You must be very excited.*

She took the paper from me and wrote, *Yes!*

*Do you like my food?*

*It's much better than the last cook's.*

*Who was the chef?*

I looked at her fingers as she passed the paper back to me. They were long and strong, and her nails were the same color as the rosemary blooms.

*An Italian guy. He didn't last long. He drank. Then we had a Japanese woman, who was very good, but she just disappeared.*

*That's bad luck. Sometimes that happens in the restaurant business, a run of bad luck and you just about have to shut your doors.* I wrote in response.

She wrote something and passed it to me.

*Do you know how to sign? I'll teach you.*

Took me a minute trying to think of the best way to explain it.

*It's my contract; I can't fraternize with family or friends.*

She shook her head, then signed her name and repeated it a couple of times in sign language until I caught on and signed *Rita* to her delight.

She scribbled another note. *I don't want to talk about rules and how things are done. I will teach you every day in the morning.*

My first lesson had ended, and she patted my hand, took the pen and paper from me, and waddled off into the inner courtyard. I glanced up and saw Security looking at me from a second-story alcove equipped with a camera and telephoto lens, studiously recording signs of my disloyalty.

Manny was right. When Monster was done with the world tour, business junket, pleasure cruise, whatever he was doing, he came back like the president landing on a carrier, sock stuffed deep into crotch. A helicopter circled the Lair a few times and settled on the great lawn in front of the manor house.

Security appeared and gestured for the staff to come out to greet the return of the conquering Monster.

He sprang from the helicopter like all the cameras in the world were focused on him, waving and beaming, wearing the biggest pair of aviator sunglasses I had ever seen and a bomber jacket that looked big enough for two of him.

He stood there giving us a stadium wave, and we waved back even though the helicopter blades kicked up a wall of stinging dust.

Security surrounded him, a circle of men in gray jumpsuits, and escorted him into the enveloping privacy of the Lair, his sanctum sanctorum.

Now that Monster had been back for a few weeks, the pressure of the job was no longer busywork, my need to appear useful even if it was a demonstration for nobody but myself.

Monster discovered my number and kept me on my toes by being demanding in this odd, jellyfish-like way. He didn't complain, didn't fire me, nothing obvious, but I felt myself being weighed down by the oddness of his needs.

For some reason he took an interest in the time the garlic was picked. Before dawn was the best, but he'd accept the hour after dusk. He needed to see my logs for substantiation. It was that important to him. That was only the beginning. Soon I was keeping extensive notes on all the herbs and vegetables I picked in the various gardens. I didn't need to know why, really. It was all about keeping everything right for Monster.

But I knew it had to do with some new age mysticism, homeopathy.

Then I realized that food to him was more like the Eucharist was for me as a child, mysterious and symbolic. Monster wanted food to transform him into something better. He needed me to be the high priest of his stomach. But then he changed up on me, wanting more variety. I guess all that juice gave him the runs.

I had to be inventive with my menus. Every now and then another note from Monster would mysteriously appear, taped onto the refrigerator by hidden kitchen operatives. That's how I received the directive to expand the Living Food menu, and for it to taste better, throwing down an impossible challenge, like imagining a five-sided square. He also pointed out how important it was for me to keep Rita from backsliding. Since she was carrying their baby, he wanted her to benefit fully from his eating regimen. Rita had spent a few days showing me the various ways to sign how much she hated the stuff. She passionately conveyed in writing how she refused to eat uncooked spaghetti squash. I agreed, and rededicated myself to making it easier on her, to break new ground with semi-living cuisine. I wanted to get to the point that she'd feel good about swallowing it, but I doubted that she would if she wanted much more than salads and cold soups. Monster liked the idea of sunbaked breads and rices for philosophical reasons. *It's so unadulterated!* he wrote in his last note.

I purchased a solar-powered glass oven that worked very well on sunny days, but on overcast days I'd just toss everything into the brick oven.

I prepared lunches for the staff too, but other than Thug's fresh steak, nothing that bled was allowed anywhere near the kitchen. I grilled on a little hibachi on a worktable near the toolshed, where I kept a small refrigerator stocked with my meats. I ate a lot of bacon, probably too much, and steak. Maybe I wanted the stink of it to annoy Monster's True Believer employees, who were happy to sustain themselves on carrot juice, ground chickpeas, and heaping teaspoons of sawdust. They wanted to be as much like Monster as possible.

I worried about Rita.

She needed a diet that wouldn't starve the baby. I read that the first thing that's affected by malnourishment is brain size. Seemed to me that any child of Monster's would need all of its faculties to have a shot at a normal life. Luckily, Santa Ynez had more kinds of goat cheese than anywhere else in California. Cheese-filled dumplings, cheese breads, and rice cheese soufflé, I made it all for her because Rita needed those calories that Monster shunned.

I THOUGHT MY RELATIONSHIP with Monster would remain the same. He'd be somewhere in the Lair, producing new music or writing, but whatever he did, I imagined that his time was so valuable he wouldn't have a moment to spare, so I was surprised when, one particularly overcast afternoon, Monster appeared in the kitchen with two blank-faced assistants whom I took to be Security without the gray jumpsuits. This was the first time I saw him close-up and in decent light. I tried not to stare at him, but it was hard; his skin glowed oddly, almost as if it were internally illuminated, and his eyes were large and beautiful, like the eyes of a girl in Japanese animation. His lank-limbed body resembled a boy's more than that of a man.

"Good morning, Mr. Stiles," I said, but Monster and his attendants watched me silently, without response. I stood with my hands dangling at my sides until it became uncomfortable and I began to feel ridiculous. I turned and picked up a handful of radishes from a green ceramic bowl and sliced them on the chopping block.

"Call me Monster," I heard from behind me, so I turned to see Monster dismiss his assistants and lean against the sink, as though he was prepared to stay a while in the kitchen.

"I want to watch you cook," he said with a smile.

I shrugged, feeling naked to his eyes. The kitchen, my kitchen, was a refuge, but with him standing there, an unwanted guest, I had to accept the fact that I was paid help, that I didn't own anything in that kitchen other than the knives I had brought with me to the Lair.

"I've been meaning to tell you I hate radishes," he said, as though it pained him.

"Sorry, I didn't know."

Monster shrugged. "Rita likes them in her salad."

"Good," I said, wondering if he had anything else he wanted to mention about my cooking.

"Don't mind me, I'm just watching you," he said, with the words hanging in the air.

"You're interested in cooking?" I asked, but Monster didn't

reply; after a moment or two I glanced up to see him still watching me like a freakish hawk. I began dicing onions and mincing herbs and started a vegetable stock, anything to keep busy.

"You know, I miss those breakfasts of toast and jam, but Mr. Chow, my herbalist, refuses to allow me to eat that anymore."

I didn't know what to say to that.

"If you don't find Living Food satisfying, you can find an alternative."

Monster shook his head.

"I've already caused so much damage to my body and spirit. Mr. Chow insists that this is my last chance to help myself achieve unity."

"Well, sometimes you need to live. If you deny yourself all the pleasures in life, it's no good, you're just torturing yourself for no reason. No one can live like that," I said, with all the earnestness of a reformed drug addict looking back at the good old days of excess.

Monster thought about it for a second, then disappeared down the hall. He returned after a few minutes and gestured for me to follow him down a grand hallway to the main entrance. There a Rolls-Royce sat idling in the long driveway.

"Let's go," he said.

Soon as the car started to move, Monster called to the driver, "Play Prince."

"You're a Prince fan?"

Monster snorted as the bass line of "Head" reverberated in the cavernous backseat. "I like *Dirty Mind*, and some of his older work. I'm not a fan of his new stuff. I just don't get it. People talk about how innovative he is, but I think I'm the one who kept up with where music is going."

I didn't want to get into a debate with Monster on that subject, but I did want to know where *we* were going since we were in such a rush, going over a hundred, blowing by traffic, racing somewhere.

When we reached the 101 and started north, I began to worry as I sat across from Monster in the seat that faces backward. I tried not to glance in Monster's direction, knowing if I did I'd be snared by him and unable to look away from the horrifically beautiful car accident that was his face.

"Where are you from?" he asked.

"I've been working in Manhattan for the last ten years," I said, looking at my hands like I was surprised to have them.

"No, where were you born?"

"I was born in Germany. My dad was in the army."

"Oh," Monster said, disappointment echoing in his voice; I guess my answer wasn't what he wanted to hear. "Did you like Germany?"

"We moved a lot, I don't remember much about the country other than it was very cold."

"Have you visited since?"

"Yes, a few times."

"How do they treat black people?"

My mind ground to a halt.

"What?"

"How do the Germans treat black people?"

"I couldn't say I noticed anything particularly racist."

"Some places don't treat black people very well. That makes me uncomfortable because some of the cats in my band, they don't get respect and that makes me angry. Russia, for instance, isn't a place I'll play again because I'd have to leave all my black personnel home, and I can't see doing that."

He paused but looked as though he was on the verge of saying something else.

I assumed he thought I was black, black man to black man, explaining the difficulty that black folks have in the world. Then for a moment I got the impression he didn't think of himself as black, and that I, with my light-skinned ass, had become the single black man in the back of the Rolls.

"My whole life I've tried to be a bridge between groups of people because I see all sides. I've evolved. I've become something different; I'm not bound by what holds people back. You see what I'm saying?"

I didn't, but I nodded anyway.

"When I was black, I couldn't see it, the big picture; then when I changed, it became clear to me and I've never looked back."

"You changed?" I asked.

"It just happened. I became something different. It happened at first internally, then the changes radiated outward. Mr. Chow said it was inevitable, that I evolved at such a fundamental level that my appearance would also reflect it."

"Well, what started it, this change?"

I realized where we were going, and at Pismo Beach we pulled off at the Arroyo Grande exit and headed for the ridiculously long line at the In-N-Out Burger.

I thought, as the Rolls idled in line, that Monster had forgotten my question, but I was wrong.

"I changed when I made my first hundred million. I wasn't black anymore, nothing was going to hold me back from finding my destiny."

I must have looked confused because he immediately began explaining himself.

"I know it sounds silly to say that once I made my money I stopped being black, but it's true. I became a different person and different rules apply to me."

I wanted to ask another question about the rules, but the driver had reached the window to order.

"Monster, what would you like?" the driver asked.

Monster clapped his hands together with childlike anticipation.

"Six orders of fries and four animal-style grilled cheeses, two vanilla shakes. You want something?" he said, nodding at me as though he'd forgotten my name.

"Just a root beer and fries."

"Good," he said. "I'm glad you're not eating cow. I can't stand that, cows are sacred to me."

I nodded in agreement, glad to make the man who paid the bills happy, but I didn't know how much happier he could be, the way he tore into that gigantic order of fast food.

Monster sat back, wiping his face with a napkin, satisfied with his large meal, Prince's "If I Was Your Girlfriend" reverberating about the cavernous interior of the Rolls as we returned to the Lair.

"You were so right, man, this is what I wanted. I owe you, Gibson. Mr. Chow needs to understand that I've got to let go and live."

I DIDN'T WANT IT TO HAPPEN, but it did. I became a kind of friend to Monster. I just wanted to work, earn money, and settle myself into the rhythm of a drug-free life, but that hope was dead. Without me being anything more than professionally friendly, Monster could not get enough of my company. He'd drop in to say hello and watch me prepare the food I knew he didn't want to eat but insisted on. I suspected that for him it was like magic, and that if he stopped with the Living Food, who knew what might happen? Maybe he'd revert, lose all the progress of that miraculous *change*, the spectacular and spontaneous event that transformed him from being a black man into a new man, a man whose color bled away until he was near albino. Is that evolution? And his hair, now that was technology, or maybe science fiction. I suspect that his hair had a mind of its own, twisting itself into a ponytail, lengthening or lightening itself whenever it got the inclination.

With a man like Monster it's hard not to become obsessed with every little detail of him, and adding up those details was an unending job.

Around him I was an anthropologist, and he was a race of one and the subject of my life's work. Reading him was worse than reading tea leaves. I had no idea what Monster thought. If he said anything at all, it was usually to complain about whatever music I played in the kitchen, though he tapped his foot to it.

Then one afternoon I watched him sample the fresh blueberries I put in front of him; he ate a few, his long white fingers staining blue, and looked up at me.

"You were married? How did that go?"

"It was good, marriage was good for me."

"Explain that."

"Explain what?

"How marriages can be good."

"I just know about my marriage, I couldn't tell you about anybody else's marriage."

"Well, can you explain why your marriage went bad?"

I shrugged. I wasn't interested in this, explaining my life to him, but I did want to know about Rita. If his relationship with her was falling apart, I wanted to know everything I could about that.

"My wife and I had a good thing going for a while and then I blew it," I said.

"Drugs?"

"Yeah."

"Was it her fault, did she lead you to drugs?"

I shook my head, "No, that disaster was all me. She didn't have a thing to do with it."

"You're lucky. Rita makes me wish I was high all the time. Sometimes I think she wants to drive me crazy. Women are like that, capable of all kinds of evilness, but I thought she was different, different from that. I was wrong, I see that now."

"What do you mean?"

Monster stood and did some fluid dance move like floating away, and then suddenly he was so close to me I took a step backward.

"You know I'm a religious man. If you're gonna bring a child into the world, you need a family, a father and mother. That's what I wanted, a real family, but I have to admit the reality, the reality is a bitch."

"If you feel like that, maybe you should get help, counseling or something."

"Oh, no, my friend. It's not me. It's her. I try to get her to see, I want her to know she's got to do better. Otherwise . . . I don't know."

I didn't have a clue of what to say to him, but he looked at me like he expected something.

"Maybe you should get somebody to talk to her. She might not understand your point of view."

"I'm a private person. I don't like dragging my business through the streets. You know how that works. All those media vultures waiting for me to slip, and camping outside the gates, waiting for the stray word on my collapsing marriage. Nothing is confidential, everybody has a price. You can bank on that. The truth is, I don't think I can make her happy. That hurts me because I do love her and she's the mother of my baby. I don't know what to do. Sometimes I think she's not into me the way she used to be. I get jealous thinking maybe she's looking for something better."

Chopping nuts to keep busy, I glanced up and he twirled again and left the kitchen so fast I almost sliced my finger off.

I WANTED THOSE MORNINGS with Rita to last, but I feared that at any moment Monster would fire me, thinking I was making a play for his wife. On the other hand, I thought maybe he didn't care, wanted her off his hands and I was doing the job for him.

Our lessons hadn't been going on for very long, but already

I longed for them, and it wasn't because I wanted to perfect my sign language skills. One afternoon, in the middle of teaching me, she reached for my hands and held my fingers and stroked each one, and though it was awkward with Security being so close, I also found it tremendously arousing. Thank God she had to leave before I reached over and kissed her.

Nights crept slowly by as I waited for sunrise and to see her again, incrementally more pregnant, enthusiastically trying to get me to the point where I could sign a basic conversation.

I knew Security watched us, looking out over the courtyard and herb garden, never a private moment. I knew I could be fired, half expected it, knew it was coming like you know that when you fall out of bed you'll hit the floor.

What could I do? She sought me out. Was I supposed to tell her no, leave me the hell alone? We sat there on the bench with her fingers blazing away and me doing my best to understand. I'd slip a glance at her breasts and want to lower my head into her cleavage and rest there for a day. One morning she took my hand and placed it on her belly.

She mouthed, "He kicks," then smiled with delight.

So, Monster was having a boy. That seemed wrong to me; maybe a girl could survive having such a strange man for a father, but a boy? I couldn't imagine Monster showing up for Saturday morning soccer, scaring the butter out of all the nannies.

She kept my hand on the drum-tight skin of her belly, and I was more than happy to have it held there.

We kissed then, briefly, our lips hardly touching. I looked up to the alcove, but Security's view was obscured by a stout avocado tree, or so I hoped.

"You are so beautiful," I whispered to her. Somehow it seemed okay that she might not be able to understand.

Maybe I didn't want that, for her to understand me. Monster might have been drawn to the same thing, not having to explain yourself with spoken words. I pulled away from her and wrote a hasty note.

*Do you have to call him Lamont or Monster?*

She laughed wordlessly and took my notebook and wrote: *What do you think I call him? I can't call him anything.*

I shrugged and wrote another note.

*When you write to him how do you refer to him? You call him Monster or Lamont?*

*Monster,* she wrote. *He is a monster. That's what he thinks of himself.*

She smiled and leaned over and kissed my lips lightly and returned to the mansion.

THERE WERE MANY THINGS I forced myself not to think about; why she was with Monster was one of them.

For his money or fame or whatever—I didn't want to know. I accepted that, at some point, Monster was the goal she had in life. Maybe she had been in a bad situation, and if she landed him, everything would make sense. I guess that bad situation changed into a fairy tale, and Monster transformed into a white knight in shining armor. It didn't last, Monster being the strange cat that he was, and Rita went back to being the needy woman. Me, I had been there; thought I could be a good husband and not the man I had been before who liked to get high. My shining armor crashed to the floor and I stood there naked to the world, a reformed basehead. And, as fucked up as I was, I had to pull myself out of that rathole of despair. If you want to help someone in a bad situation, you need to give them the opportunity to work their way out of it. At least that's how it was for me, and with the help of Asha I managed to pull myself out of the mess of my life. But it wasn't Asha dragging me by the scruff of my neck to independence from drugs. It was me; I wanted to stop. I wouldn't ruin that for Rita, snatching away that last shred of dignity, even if it made me feel good about myself, like I was some kind of half-assed hero on a mission to save wayward white women. I didn't need to know her personal tragedy, character flaw, failing, or whatever it was that led her to Monster's Lair. She was down that path and so was I, and now the future was more important than rehashing the past.

I PICKED UP Marvin Gaye's *What's Going On* in a cutout bin at a gas station in Solvang.

If I couldn't sleep, I'd listen to Marvin relentlessly until I passed out, drunk off his voice. He had his demons, but his soul was made pure by the suffering that even a deaf fool could hear in his voice; he became my companion in misery. He made nights bearable. Before, I'd lie in bed listening to crickets until the crickets got tired of putting on a show, and I'd get sick of myself and think that this was why I became a basehead, not being able to stand myself. I wanted to get to a better place, a quiet place, a place very much like Monster's Lair, a high that isolated you from all the madness and noise until you realized none of it made sense, that you were fucked. The pipe will do that for you, make the mundane bullshit of everyday life disappear, to be replaced by the monumental bullshit of looking for the next high.

I could have written a book on how I was slowly becoming a roach, giving up my humanity for the constant thrill of the pipe, the allure and squalor of it.

Dreams of Rita receded into the fatigue of sleeplessness, and I couldn't force myself to stay awake; when my growing fascination/minor obsession with Monster couldn't sustain me and Marvin couldn't help me, I'd drift off to a dead sleep, usually and thankfully free of dreams, but not tonight.

Tonight I heard gunshots.

I heard them distinctly and they were near. I had an innate instinct not to get too excited by gunshots, and of course I didn't make the suburban mistake of flinging the door open to see what was happening. I pulled a pillow over my head and hoped that whatever it was would end, but it didn't. I heard stout voices shouting, and more shots, and the endlessly shining lights of Monster's Lair blazed brighter. They invaded my bungalow, casting shadows, making everything disorienting. From behind the bungalow a commotion erupted, shouts and curses, the sounds of a struggle.

Panicked, I rushed for the door, flung it open, and ran down the steps of the bungalow, and before I could decide where to run next, I heard a command to freeze.

"Don't move!"

I stopped and held my arms high. Blinded by the lights, all I could do was squint in the directions of the voices.

"Is that him? I thought we had that son of a bitch."

"No," another voice replied. "He's the cook."

"Go inside and stay," the voice shouted.

I did as they asked. I sat in the rocking chair with a blanket wrapped around me, and listened to them shout as they searched for the intruder until just about daybreak. Was this the same intruder who had been mentioned earlier? He had found a way onto the grounds and caused a DEFCON 1 kind of reaction, even with all the security upgrades. I felt kind of giddy with excitement and I wasn't sure why, other than I guess I liked the idea of Monster's kingdom besieged.

Early the next morning Monster appeared in the kitchen,

sporting a fuzzy purple robe and matching slippers and a bone-colored stocking cap over his jet-black hair. He reminded me of actor Claude Rains in a smoking jacket, wrapped in white, wrapped ready to unroll and disappear in an instant.

"You heard that craziness outside of your bungalow?" Monster asked as he ran his hand over the purple fuzz of his robe.

I shook my head. "It wasn't a problem. I could have slept through it, but these days I don't sleep well."

Monster laughed. "You don't have to lie. I heard the situation got ugly. I need to fire somebody, madness just keeps going on and I can't convey to Security how important it is to roll up this intruder."

"Who?"

His eyes flared.

"My stalker. He comes with the job. You don't get to be a true superstar without a stalker trying to get into your life. You catch one and there's another popping up like a fucking jack-in the-box."

I had never seen Monster pissed off; his cheeks had an unnatural ruddiness to them, and he shook his head, unable to calm himself.

"I hate my life when it gets like this, when I can't control what happens. I can't live like that. I can't do good work when my head is about to explode."

"Security had the stalker under control, but somehow he got free. I thought they would have him arrested by now."

Monster scowled.

"I'm not talking about that idiot, he's just a humbug. I let it get out of hand because I don't want to get nasty, and that's the only reason he gets away with what he does. When I'm ready, it's done like a fucking baked potato."

Monster had got himself so agitated that he had to wipe his mouth with the back of the sleeve of his robe.

"You know the stalker?"

"Hell, yeah! I know him, but I'm not talking about that. I'm talking about the stupid business I'm in. Dealing with those fuckers just makes me insane. Like my time isn't valuable. They don't respect me and I'm the one making money for them, the greedy fuckers."

"It must be difficult working with people like that."

"Oh, no, you don't have a clue. You need to see these dogs in action. Slavery is still in effect."

Monster paused and looked at me.

"Yeah, get ready, we're flying to LA at noon," he said.

"Los Angeles? You want me to go to Los Angeles with you?"

"Yes. I need you. Thug isn't back and I need another set of eyes."

"Okay," I said, wishing I knew what I was getting myself into. Monster rushed out of the kitchen as if his stocking-covered hair was on fire.

AFTER I PREPARED BREAKFAST and sent it up, I wondered if I should have lunch ready for Monster and this trip to Los Angeles. I decided to be safe and not sorry, and made spring rolls and a fruit salad and wondered whether to stay in the kitchen or to wait out front by the driveway. I changed into a black turtleneck and washed my face. It just seemed silly to wait outside with a wicker basket to catch a ride with Monster, like some bedraggled day laborer. I stepped out of the restroom and glanced at my watch: ten to noon and I still couldn't decide what to do.

The door to the kitchen opened and Security entered, the tall one. He gestured for me to follow him. I started to, and then he noticed my basket.

"What's in there?" he asked gruffly.

"Monster's lunch."

"You have cutlery in there?"

"I have one knife to cut fruit and some forks. Is that a problem?"

Security squinted for a second, then turned away and called someone on his walkie-talkie for a short but intense conversation, then turned back to me.

"Leave it. We have serving utensils."

I shrugged and placed the knife on the cutting block. Then Security gestured for me to hand him the basket. He rustled through it, opening containers until he was satisfied, and handed it back. I didn't understand; I could cook for him at the Lair, but anywhere else they would treat me like a potential assassin? He gestured for me to follow him, and we walked around to the driveway and then past that to the big expanse of lawn. Monster stood with his arms folded beneath the umbrella held by the outstretched arm of more Security. Monster was resplendent in white: from shoes to suit to the white scarf around his head, capping off with a white fedora. Preoccupied, he didn't acknowledge my arrival; for a long awkward moment we waited for something, and I wasn't sure what. I looked up to the sound of thumping and the sight of a helicopter churning air, and I realized how we would be getting to Los Angeles.

The four of us boarded the helicopter, which could seat ten easily, but Monster sat up front near the pilot and immediately began to question him about wind conditions. To my surprise, Monster was the one who guided the helicopter into the air. Monster had to be flight-trained, though I felt pretty fucking uncomfortable with him piloting the helicopter. We arrived in Santa Monica within an hour and fifteen minutes. The pilot took the controls from Monster and landed us on the roof of a low-slung office building.

As we disembarked, Monster turned to me with a frown. "The best thing about this fucking trip is I get to log more helicopter hours."

Security followed Monster with multiple briefcases in each hand. Carrying only the wicker basket, I felt I had got off easy because some poor fool had to lug Monster's portable wardrobe, rolling it after him like it was his clumsy tail. Outside of the radius of the slowing helicopter blades were at least a half dozen pensive suits, some black, most white, all dressed expensively and conservatively, except for the man at the head of the pack, who wore a silk T-shirt that couldn't restrain his girth. He sported many tattoos, blocky Chinese characters that ran along the length of his arms, and a malevolent grin on his face as he approached Monster with an outstretched hand.

"Yo, man, finally got your lazy ass down here."

Monster reluctantly extended his hand, and the fat man enveloped Monster in an all-encompassing hug. Monster looked lost and hopeless as he struggled to disengage himself from the fat man's embrace.

A member of Security stepped forward, maybe a little too close because the fat man slapped him in the face.

"Don't be walking up on me, bitch," he said.

Red-faced, Security stepped back, but his job was done. Monster was freed, and surrounded by his own Security and stunned executives.

"Come on, y'all. We got work to do," the fat, light-skinned guy said. But Monster no longer looked intimidated or overwhelmed.

"Hey, Syn, don't slap my people. Don't you dare do shit like that."

Syn laughed, amused with Monster's rage. "Look at you, getting all hard. I'm almost scared of your skinny ass."

Several executives stepped between them and then led us into the building. Once inside, I saw that we were at a recording studio, sound engineers and techs hurrying around, rushing back and forth behind glass partitions. The decor resembled a ski lodge from the seventies with all of that wood paneling and indoor ivy and ferns galore.

I maneuvered around Security (and they weren't happy about that) to whisper a question to Monster.

"Who's the fat guy?"

Monster took off his sunglasses to reveal his brilliantly blue contacts and frowned. "That's Syn, the most overpaid producer in the business."

"Damn straight. That's why they got me working with you," Syn said, overhearing Monster. " 'Cause you need me, brotha. You know you need me. I got the skills to take you to the next level."

That comment enraged Monster, to Syn's continued delight.

"I don't need you. These idiots are paying you, not me. There's not a fucking thing you can teach me. And you need to get this straight, I'm not your brotha."

"Then what are you?"

"Whatever, just not your brotha."

"I'm asking, then what are you? You white, bitch? 'Cause you bleach yourself, you the white man? Be for real!"

Faster than I imagined Monster could move, he wheeled around and his hand darted toward Syn's face and clawed him, brutally. Bloody on one cheek and across the forehead, Syn touched at the scratches and flinched. I imagined he wanted to beat the shit out of Monster, and Security would have a hell of a time stopping him. He took a deep breath and reached into his pocket for a handkerchief, which he pressed against his face.

"Unless you get with me, your shit is over. I'm the one you need."

Monster waved off Syn and hurried away, executives rushing after him like he was the pied piper. Security directed me to wait in a reception area with rough-hewed furniture, a bearskin rug, and a gigantic fireplace, big enough for four men to walk in and have room to stretch—more ski-lodge chic. I sat down in front of the fireplace, needing a brandy or a whiskey, really anything.

"So, who the fuck are you? You look a little old to be hanging with Monster."

"What?" I turned to see Syn standing there with the handkerchief still pressed against his face and a cigarette in his free hand.

"And you ain't blond."

"I don't know what you're talking about."

"Oh, so you saying you never noticed Monster's taste. Cool, I'm believing you."

"I just started working for him. I'm not in the loop and don't know what you're talking about."

"Yeah, well, you gonna know soon. See, you look kinda normal, not all fugazi, and you ain't that lunatic he usually has with him, so I thought I'd try talking at you."

"What lunatic?"

"That fool, his bodyguard, Thug."

"Thug. I know who he is.

"Yeah, he's a big muthafucking thug, and Thug is that fool's name. 'Cause if you met him, you'd remember his ass. You don't forget Thug."

"Yeah, I remember him. Think it might be impossible to forget him."

Syn looked me up and down. "If you into that. I don't have a problem with what people do, but that sure as hell ain't me, that fool ain't even on the down low, he straight up high about it."

He shook his head like he didn't know what to think of me, whether I was Thug's lover or just stupid.

"So, why you and Monster have bad blood between you?"

Syn shrugged and walked over to the fireplace and looked inside.

"I hate his ass, and he hates me, but shit's got to come out. We need to get this done, but he spends all the time trying to get me fired. But them executives don't think Monster got shit to say. He did when I was in diapers, but not now. His shit's been weak for a while, but that's on him. I'm about to move on, and a whole lot of money is gonna get wasted. The shit is kinda funny, if you look at it like that. See, I could break that little freak easy, but I'm already on probation and then, you know, I don't want to be having to fuck with Thug. I ain't no coward, but that shit is suicide."

I heard a commotion down the hall, and there was Monster rushing for the exit of the building. I followed him out, and soon we were back on the helicopter, beating it back to Monster's Lair.

Monster sat back among the passengers, obviously too upset to fly. He sipped a carrot juice, but from the expression on his face it had to be something more than carrot juice; his shoulders sagged and he sighed. With the Pacific Ocean, flashing by outside the helicopter, framing his head, Monster explained it, ran it down to me.

"I don't care if they spent a million for studio time and that fuckup Syn. It's me; it's what I want to do. The sun rises and sets because I say so. They need to understand that, or they'll never see another album from me. Do you know what I'm saying? Do you feel me?"

I looked at him, at those sunglasses that hid those blue contacts, and nodded like I knew what the hell he was getting at.

"I put food on their tables; I pay for their cars and their children's educations. All these fucking leeches should know they don't know shit other than I'm the man, the meal ticket. They can't tell me shit. If I never make another dollar, I would have made more money for them than they'll ever make from anybody else. But these people don't have gratitude because they're not really human. Dogs at least treat the man who brings them a bone with a little respect, but not these fools. I give all I can, and they want more from me, or else they'll bring another cat in to replace me, but it can't be done. I know that for a fact, more than anything else, that they can't replace me."

Monster sat back, exhausted from explaining himself. Well, at least about the music I understood him; I got the sense that Monster was the goose that laid the golden egg, and if his laying days were over, he was cooked. I opened the wicker basket and served him a spring roll. He ate in silence until he looked at me once more.

"See, that's all I'm asking for, to be treated with respect, that's it. Like you did, you did your job. That's all I'm asking for. Don't treat me like an idiot, and try to force me to work with frauds pretending they've got skills when it's obvious they don't have shit."

I had never been more satisfied to serve someone a spring roll. Monster sighed and closed his eyes, and I looked out at the ocean, happy to be earning my money.

A week later, one bright, unusually warm morning, when bees and hummingbirds darted about the Mexican sage and flowering cabbage, Rita didn't come to the herb garden to meet me for our sign language lesson.

The baby had been born.

I sat on the bench and practiced signing her name, but it wasn't any good without her sitting next to me, fingers conjuring words far faster than I could discern them. Of course Security was there to keep me company, observing from the second-floor alcove.

I didn't care.

Then the great door of the manor house opened, and Monster stepped outside onto the grounds, wearing a big-brimmed hat and gloves and carrying an open umbrella.

He walked light-footed in a broad circle toward the distant oaks, then around to the rose gardens. Finally he saw me.

"Gibson," he said, pausing.

"Hello," I said. "How's it going?"

I couldn't see his eyes, hidden in the shadow of his hat, behind sunglasses.

He reminded me of this albino black kid I knew growing up. He'd come outside in broad daylight without hat or gloves or anything, squinting even in the late afternoon, but at noon he'd be out there too, wincing, his pinkish-white skin blistering in the direct sun. If he lucked out and found some shade, he'd linger in it, but mostly he fought the sun, and the sun won. The boy looked like somebody had set him on a slow roast and had forgotten to turn the oven off. After reddish-black welts appeared on his skin, discoloring the thin, peach-colored fuzz of his short Afro, he was condemned to stay indoors. Then the house of his foster parents caught fire, the result of him torching his bedroom because he wanted to blacken it like he wanted to blacken his skin.

"I wanted you to know that Rita had the baby this morning. She's doing well," Monster said.

"That's great. What did she have?"

"A boy. I named him King Rex Stiles."

I nodded, uncomfortably standing there, trying to reconcile Rita being with him with the reality of him. We stood out there until I awkwardly turned away. I guess he was staring at me, but I couldn't be sure with his sunglasses on.

Was he going to name the boy King Rex? Was he joking?

"I want you to make a cake. A birthday cake."

"Anything in particular?"

I was sure he was going to ask for a Living Food cake, imagining a mound of uncooked rice flour with a white, sugarless, gelatinous icing.

"Oh, something silly. With balloons, something really sweet and delicious."

"What kind of frosting would you like?"

"Rita likes chocolate. You can make it chocolate with raspberry filling."

I wondered if he wanted to lick the bowl. Then he surprised me and took off the sunglasses. He squinted and took his time staring at me, like it was the first time he'd got a good look at me.

The placid smile he wore seemed tattooed onto his face.

"Rita likes you. She gets so lonely. Sometimes I can't get her to get beyond that loneliness. I'm gone so much on business I can't do much to help her. Now that we have the baby, I hope she'll be happier because I don't know how much more I can take of her attitude."

"That's great," I said. "How many should the cake serve?"

Monster thought for a minute.

"A small cake. I don't want to get fat," he said, sliding his hands along the concaveness of his stomach.

"Sure, I'll put something together."

He looked at me for a moment and took a step back, like he finally saw the roundness of my nose, the shape of my face. Might I actually be a black man?

Then he composed himself, smiled, and turned around to leave.

"Gibson, you're doing a good job," he said over his shoulder as he vanished into the mansion.

## CURED FLUKE WITH AVOCADO, CITRUS SUPREMES, AND TOKYO TURNIPS

SERVES 4

TOKYO TURNIPS

½ cup extra-virgin olive oil (EVOO)
¼ teaspoon sugar
1 shallot, chopped
¼ teaspoon coriander
Sea salt and ¼ teaspoon white pepper
4 (or more) Tokyo turnips

AVOCADO MOSAICS

2 ripe Hass avocados
3 tablespoons lemon juice

FLUKE

1 cup sea salt
1 cup sugar
Zest and juice of 3 limes
Zest and juice of 3 Meyer lemons
Zest and juice of 2 blood oranges
1 fluke fillet, enough for 4 portions

FOR PLATING

Citrus supremes (wedges with all pith removed)
Micro cilantro
Jalapeño peppers, sliced into thin rounds
Dill sprigs
Candied lemon zest

*Prepare the Tokyo turnips:* In a bowl, mix the EVOO, sugar, shallot, coriander, and salt and pepper. Put the mixture into a ziplock bag with the turnips, squeezing out as much air as possible. Seal the bag and marinate the turnips for at least 1 hour.

*Make the avocado mosaics:* Scoop the avocado flesh out of the rinds. Put it and the lemon juice in a ziplock bag; close the bag; and, using the back of a ladle, crush the mixture until flat. Put it in the freezer for 1 hour. Then use a 3-inch-diameter cookie cutter to make shapes.

*Cure the fluke:* Mix the salt, sugar, zests, and juices. Cover the fluke with the mixture and cure for 15 minutes.

*To plate:* For each portion, place a slice of fluke and a turnip on an avocado mosaic with citrus supreme. Top with cilantro, jalapeño rounds, dill, and candied lemon zest.

# CHAPTER FIVE

I RECEIVED A LETTER FROM ELENA, BUT happy and excited as I was to receive it, I couldn't open it on a break in the kitchen, or even later in my bungalow. I couldn't bring myself to open it even when I was on a walk around the grounds.

On the beach in Pismo, warming in the sun, stripping off my clothes and plunging into the frigid Pacific and swimming to the buoys, coming back too exhausted to feel bitter disappointment, is where I wanted to be when I opened the letter. I didn't want to rush because I was ecstatic to have a connection with her, and as soon as I opened that envelope and read whatever she had to say, I was fairly sure I'd be back down to earth; below it, even. It couldn't be good news, the news that I wanted to hear, that she wanted me back, wanted to start over. No, it would be fucked-up news, the shit of divorce. More papers to be signed, more money that needed to be paid now that I was working.

I put the letter in my jacket pocket and waited for Friday and my day off. I'd catch a ride down the hill with Manny and put my plan into effect. I'd had a lot to keep me distracted. Monster was entertaining another onslaught of celebrity friends for a political fund-raiser for a Teutonic senatorial candidate. I didn't have much to do with the planning, other than providing meals for Monster and Rita, and anybody else who was interested in the Living Food manifesto. The caterers handled the rest, but it turned out that these caterers were insanely incompetent. I sat down with them and looked at what they intended to do and the prices they wanted to charge and I fired them right there. The man, blond and effeminate, and his partner, a dark-haired, overweight woman, didn't seem angry. I guess they figured Monster would unfire them, and sure enough, they were right. I left a detailed note for Monster about my opinion on the subject of the caterers and went back to my bungalow. It was almost dark, right before the floodlights kicked in and Monster's Lair would get lit up like a used car lot. I had just unlocked my door and stepped into the bungalow, when I heard a noise and quickly found the light switch.

A muscular, dark-skinned man lay stretched out on my bed. I bet it was Thug, Monster's assistant.

"Gibson," he said without expression. "What's up, dog?"

"I thought I had the only key to my bungalow."

Thug nodded. "Don't trip. Your door was unlocked and I thought I'd come in and kick it with you."

I wasn't interested in his explanation. He didn't have a right to break into my room and I was righteously pissed and showed it, but Thug played like he didn't notice.

"I thought we were cool, you and me. I'm the reason you got the job."

"Really," I said, with surprise. "You're into this Living Food thing?"

"Naw, I hate that crap. You'd never see me put that bullshit in my mouth."

"But you hired me, you must know about haute cuisine."

"Hell, no. I could give a fuck about that. Shit, I wish they had an In-N-Out Burger around here."

"You'd have to drive to Arroyo Grande," I said, trying to be helpful.

"I told Monster you were cool because you knew what you were talking about on the phone and Bridget said you had a famous restaurant and all that until you had got into a little drug fiending. But that's the past and I'm not hating. If you had problems, you ain't the first and you won't be the last. You feeling me?"

I shrugged.

"But this ain't about that."

"What's it about?"

"It's about us."

My heart stopped beating for a second.

"See, I thought, you know, maybe we'd hook up," he said, smoothly, almost in a whisper.

I was glad to hear that he was asking me to hook up and not telling me we were hooking up. I'd had some awful jobs in my life and paid my share of dues, but I didn't plan to pay that kind of dues.

"Look, Thug, I'm not into hooking up and all. I'm a married man."

He kept smiling as though he wasn't listening to me. His hands were huge. I wouldn't want to fight him without a bat in my hands, and even then I'm not sure it would be fair. I crossed the room to where the fireplace tools were. I didn't reach for the poker, but it felt good to have it near at hand.

"I appreciate you doing all that for me. I'll buy you a beer or something."

Thug laughed boyishly and stretched out on the bed.

"Gibson, you and me, we need to talk."

"Yeah, well, we're talking now."

"Yeah, you right. But we need to quit all this bullshit and really just kick back and talk."

Thug wore this gigantic Joe Montana throwback jersey, as if Joe were big as Shaq. In one quick move he slipped the jersey over his head and tossed it to the floor. He had no flab beneath that jersey, nothing but black buffed muscle.

"Why you gonna be like that?"

Thug's dark skin glistened against the white sheets as if he had oiled himself before this so-called chance encounter.

I panicked as his hands reached for the buttons of his ridiculous Sean John jeans. If he slid his pants down, I'd grab the poker, though grabbing the poker suddenly seemed very embarrassing.

"Don't look so hard like you gonna try to beat me down."

I nodded silently, praying he would leave.

"I know all about your thing with Rita. I got photographs."

"Know what? There's nothing to know."

The big man sat up and leaned forward for a manila envelope and reached inside. In his hand he held grainy blowups of me and Rita.

"That's a nice one of you two kissing. I haven't shown that to Monster. I don't think he needs to know."

"That was my fault. She didn't want to. I took advantage of her."

Thug laughed. "What? You supposed to be a hero or something? All kind of shit goes on here. You think she ain't getting paid? That's why we're all here, Monster pays from a big roll of bills and we're all lined up with our hands out, even you, my brother. Rita's getting paid, paid enough so she'll never worry about money even if she lives to be one hundred and fifty."

"Paid? Isn't she supposed to be his wife?"

Thug laughed again, like he wanted the whole world to know he was amused.

"Do you really think Monster is into women? Shit, he's about as interested in bitches as I am. But that's not true. I've had my share, and I've got a couple kids to prove it, but I'd bet my life that Monster has never been with a woman."

I sighed, thinking of Rita.

"So, what I'm saying is don't be naive. We're all in this for the same reason." Then Thug's seriousness faded and the smile returned. He was ready to get down to business.

"It's too bad about you not having an open mind 'cause we could have had us a good time," he said, with a big countrified grin.

"Sorry, Thug. Look, I'm not putting you down or anything."

"Cool. Just keep grilling my steaks. Monster wants me to get into that Living Food bullshit. I'd starve first."

He stood up to leave and laughed when he saw my hand on the poker.

"One thing I need to know before I bail up out of here."

"Yeah," I said, waiting for the question, but Thug took his time, crossing and uncrossing his arms.

"So what's with you passing for white? First time I saw you I knew you was a nigga."

"Who said I was passing?"

"You ain't?"

"No, man. I am what I am."

"What, you Popeye or something?"

"What's that supposed to mean?"

Thug shrugged and walked toward me. I stepped aside, and he turned and lingered in the doorway, eyeing me.

"First, Monster thought you were a Jew. He used to like Jews. Now, he has problems with them. I said you were cool, you weren't a Jew. He looked right over the fact that you were black. I mean, you are light, lighter than a lot of white people with tans, but still Monster used to be up on that. He'd say, No way! Don't be hiring black people, I don't care if they look white."

"Why?"

Thug laughed thunderously.

"Do I look like a psychiatrist? All I know is I'm the only real black man working for that crazy muthafucka. I thought I could slip you in since Monster didn't notice you, or didn't care."

"Thanks, I guess."

"I thought we had something big in common," Thug said, and grabbed at his crotch. I took a step backward.

"I don't want to disappoint you, but I'm just average on a good day."

"Let me be the judge of that," he said.

I retreated another step. Thug finally gave up on his

heavy-handed seduction and stepped outside into the brightly lit night of Monster's Lair.

After Thug left, I put a chair beneath the doorknob and slept in the recliner near the fireplace, leaving pillows under the sheets for Thug to interfere with if he decided to bum-rush the show.

Morning came and I was out of the bungalow with a backpack stuffed with everything I could possibly need for a day away.

Manny blew the horn of his pickup and I hurried outside and hopped in.

"My friend, you stay away from this Thug. He is unnatural. A *pato*."

"A duck?"

"Yes, a *pato*."

He dropped me off at the beach and said he'd give me a ride back the next day when he returned from Lompoc. Lompoc was another strange California name that sounded like a disease, a rare form of smallpox or something. Anyway, it was a town I didn't plan to visit, even if it was the Cut Flower Capital of the United States and the vast fields of flowers were supposed to be spectacular.

I arrived at the motel and immediately put on my trunks, grabbed a skinny towel, and ran straight for the ocean. I dived in without hesitation, though it was an overcast day.

Frigid!

I tried swimming out somewhere near the distant buoys, but I didn't get close.

My stroke was fucked up and then the chill got to me, so cold my testicles headed north, lost in the maze of my lower intestines. I turned around and pounded the water until I dragged my sorry ass out of the surf and collapsed onto my towel.

Frigid fingers fumbled with the envelope, ripping the letter as it pulled free.

*Gibson—*

*We need to talk, work through our issues. I'm ready for a face-to-face. Hope you are well.*

*Love,*

*Elena*

A firebomb went off in my chest, air rushed from my lungs, gasping for breath on dry land.

Dazzling images of the perpetual happiness of marriage: sharing a bed, a shower, breakfast, a return to a life I had never expected to have again, a life with her. I was high on it, higher than I had ever been on the pipe.

Exile was over. Elena was calling me home.

It took a day for Asha to return my call; she had one emergency after another to handle back there at the halfway house. Meth freaks were in revolt. Mistake was that they sent her three, and in a program for ten, three tweakers were ten times too many. Crackheads and heroin addicts were more or less manageable, but not meth freaks, or so she told me. They were always irritable, belligerent, or withdrawn, and of course they regularly relapsed, which meant a hell of a lot of paperwork.

"I wish you were here," she said, laughing. "At least I never had to worry about the kitchen."

We laughed about that, the good old days of life in a halfway house, slinging gruel for the semi-institutionalized.

Then I told her about the letter.

"Oh, that's great, that's wonderful news."

"I want to come back to New Jersey."

Asha was quiet on the other end.

"Did you talk to your parole officer?"

"Not yet."

Asha sighed.

"Bridget will kill me if you leave."

"I thought she intended to quit."

Asha sighed.

"She can't find another position, and she can't bring herself to walk out on her contract."

"Everything is so fucking complicated," I said.

"Let me talk to Bridget. Maybe we can work something out. What did you say to Elena?"

My heart sank. I imagined it would be difficult, but I

didn't want to face up to it. I wasn't ready to talk to her. I wanted to be sure of how things were going to go with me before contacting her. I didn't want to blow it, didn't want her turning her back on me once again, because I was sure of one thing: that would beat me down and keep me down for good.

"I'm not ready to talk to her yet. I don't want to say something stupid and ruin it."

Asha laughed. "Gibson, don't be so hard on yourself. Call her. Let her know what's going on. It'll change everything."

"You really believe that?"

"As the patron saint of lost causes, I've got to believe."

"Oh, yeah. I forgot about that. You save souls and all that."

"Like any good Hindu should."

MY LIFE WAS STUCK between the pages of a book I couldn't wait to be done with. Funny to be so unhappy in a place so fucking beautiful. From the mountain you could see the Pacific Ocean curving away, vanishing into the blue horizon and the grid-like vineyards on the hills below; or, in the afternoon sun, the undulations of hillsides resembling the contours of a body in repose. Sure, I wanted to wake up and breathe air so fresh it made my head hurt, taste water so fresh it was sweet, but not here, not doing this job, away from the woman I loved.

This was Monster's heaven, but not just his, also those

who shared his idea of heaven, a valley of vintners, cheese makers, developers, and cattle barons. It made me want to take a shit in somebody's winding driveway.

Why couldn't there be a smoke-filled bar that played something other than country music or the Eagles in this whole fucking county?

Once, on my way to the weekly farmer's market in Solvang, I saw blond children biking alongside the road, cell phones clutched to their ears, and I began to understand this rarefied life. And even more so when I watched a ramshackle barn quickly converted into an understatedly charming home with the big satellite dish, for the thin but not anorexic mom canning homegrown preserves. Her children deserved the freshest bread, the best organic produce, while her husband tooled around in a gigantic SUV, examining his endless rows of grapevines. They lived in an alternative universe, another kind of American dream, outrageously expensive but a return to the heavily amended, composted earth. The charm of this upscale, gentlemanly farming was for folks who didn't want to be too much with the land, wanted it on their terms, hands not too deep in the fecund earth, walking lightly upon the fields, breathing good air, alongside Mexican workers who might dream the same dreams but couldn't afford them in this life, maybe not even the next.

Isolation made me judgmental in temperament when before I was wildly indifferent, ignoring everything that was outside of my concern: food preparation, presentation, and money.

Money like honey.

I wanted to be back East, for the good summer heat and humidity of New York. Seeing brown, black, and white skin sweating in the hot sun as people walked down teeming sidewalks. I wanted to smell the rankness of the discards from the fish market, the vegetables rotting in trash bins.

I wanted to be too much with the world, not living this life of seclusion among folks hiding in fortresses of wealth and abundance. I wanted the Manhattan version, where the wealth was vertical, not horizontal.

And I was horny, horny enough to gnaw through wood.

I wanted to be back with Elena, fucking like minks, making up for what we lost. For the first time in a long time I was content to be in my skin. Life was worth living, with the promise of a future I could believe in.

## GRILLED LOWER EAST SIDE STRIP STEAK WITH SPUN HERBS

SERVES 4

SPUN HERB PUREE

½ bunch cilantro, rinsed
½ bunch parsley, rinsed
3 cloves garlic
Zest of 1 Meyer lemon
1 cup extra-virgin olive oil (EVOO)

STEAKS

Four 8-ounce 1-inch-thick New York strips, at room temperature
Oil, for brushing the grill
Truffle salt
Freshly ground black pepper
1 lemon

*Make the spun herb puree:* Combine all the ingredients in a blender and process until smooth. Set aside.

*Make the steaks:* To avoid sticking, clean the grill and brush it with oil. Heat the grill.

Season the steaks liberally. When the grill is smoking hot, place the steaks directly on it. After about 3 minutes, rotate each steak 45 degrees to the left, making grill diamonds. Then turn the steaks over and leave for another 4 to 5 minutes. Remove them from the grill and—this is mandatory—let them rest for 10 minutes.

Spread the spun herb puree over the steaks and squeeze fresh lemon juice on top. Steezapetit!

# CHAPTER SIX

IT MUST HAVE BEEN ABOUT 6:00 A.M., when I started breakfast, when Manny appeared, knocking madly at the kitchen door. The rule was Monster liked to eat at 7:00 a.m., so I had more than enough time to prepare his diet of toast and jam and butter. Monster seemed to have loosened the grip of the Living Food manifesto, so Rita and the staff ate more balanced meals and breakfasts. The menu had expanded to omelets and potatoes and the like.

Manuel had dropped me off at my bungalow so I could change and shave, but less than five minutes later he returned, pounding on my door. I threw it open, and he stood there rattling off in rapid Spanish about a disaster. I could barely keep up with him as we hurried along the path to the main estate.

Ten yards away I saw a boy's naked body sprawled like spilled paint on the brilliantly green expanse of lawn.

We stopped a good distance away. He looked to be about eighteen, with long blond hair framing his handsome face and blue unseeing eyes, and that was enough for me. I glanced away, afraid and ashamed.

"Did you call somebody?"

"Yes," Manuel said, his voice trembling.

"Security?"

"*Sí.*"

I looked around, feeling exposed. Security wasn't to be seen, and those motherfuckers lurked about like flies on horseshit. Where were they?

"Manuel, do you have a lawyer?"

"No, what would I need with a lawyer?"

I shook my head. "Trust me, you are going to need one. We both will."

In the distance I could see a pair of black-and-whites making the turn onto the road that wove up to Monster's Lair.

I forced myself to look at him again; he looked so boyish. His face was bluish, but other than that he didn't seem to have obvious injuries.

After I opened my eyes and forced myself to really look at him—his arms, then his feet, blood beaded between the toes of one foot—it was obvious: he had overdosed, or somebody had overdosed him.

The police drove across the lawn and stopped. As if on

cue, Security appeared out of thin air, with their silly uniforms and blank faces of authority.

They converged on us as though a trap had sprung, a trap for really slow-witted fools who should have seen themselves getting set up.

Security watched as the police rushed over with drawn guns. We both held our hands high into the air and let the police roughly pull them down and behind our backs to handcuff us.

GRAVES WAS THE NAME of the big blond man who interrogated me in one of the many rooms of the Security bungalow. He seemed friendly enough, and took his time with his leading questions, some of which weren't very leading.

"Did you know the boy?"

I shook my head.

"Do you like boys?"

I wanted to laugh, but I knew better.

"No, I don't like boys. I don't like children in general. I don't have much to do with children and I don't go out of my way to associate with them."

"Witnesses place you with the boy."

"I never saw him before."

He looked as though he couldn't decide if I was smart enough to lie intelligently.

"How about I search your bungalow? Do you have a problem with that, or do I need to get a search warrant?"

What did I have in that apartment other than a couple of cookbooks I'd picked up used at the Solvang swap meet and my collection of *Penthouses* and *Playboys*?

"I don't care."

"What do you think was done to the boy?" he asked me with one eyebrow cocked.

I shrugged, but then I guess my experience as a former junkie and graduate of a diversion program came into play. I itched to talk when I knew I should keep my mouth shut.

"I think somebody overdosed him."

Graves cocked an eyebrow.

"Why?"

"His feet. Check out his toes. Someone shot him up there. Maybe he did it himself, but you'd have to wonder."

Now, the sheriff looked uncomfortable. My having a brain and a potentially useful observation changed the dynamic between us.

"Security here showed me your file. You're on probation?"

I nodded and told him the name of my probation officer.

"I had a problem, but I've been clean for over a year."

Sheriff Graves closed his notebook and stood up and extended his hand.

"Mr. Gibson, you'll have to stay in the area if we need to contact you for further interviews."

"Sure. I'm not going anywhere."

"Good," he said, and walked me to the door.

MONSTER'S LAIR IS A VAST PIECE of property. Monster is the master of all he surveys, and anything else of interest, he'll get around to owning that too. If you examine his property holdings on a map, you might suspect he was buying concentric circles of privacy, ending in that moat that isolated the inner mansion, the castle keep of Monster's Lair. I had to take my hat off to his foresight. His world was besieged with swarming media drones doing their best to break on through, but they couldn't. He had them beat. Two hours hadn't passed since we'd discovered the body and they were everywhere; newscasters and cameramen clustered near the guard shack, cut off by gates, fences, and distance, and the narrow road that presented the only access to the main property, a road that seemed to have been chosen with military considerations, was closed. From Monster's Lair you could see everything approaching, exposed on that three-mile drive straight up. We were unassailable by land.

It was as if he'd known something would happen: A boy's body would be found in broad daylight on his property, and a media feeding frenzy would commence. And, as Monster intended, those media assholes would splat like bugs against the great windshield of Security.

But the police couldn't be denied, and more and more of them arrived. That was the first time I saw anyone enter the inner lair of Monster's Lair through the main entrance. Sheriff Graves, a broad-stepping man in cowboy boots, unintimidated by Monster's celebrity, strode up to the door and didn't bother to ring but used a beefy hand to pound a few times before Security opened it. He disappeared inside, and soon the sight of anyone but Monster's most trusted staff in the inner sanctum of the Lair became less interesting. Within an hour, Graves and his men passed in and out at least a half dozen times.

He was the ranking officer as far as I could see; clutches of officers circled about him, discussing the game plan of the investigation.

I was relieved to seclude myself in the kitchen, but returned outside when I heard the thumping of a helicopter circling relentlessly overhead. In response, powerful hoses appeared, manned by Security and aimed at the low-flying media helicopter, until it retreated to a safer and drier altitude.

The disconcerting thing about living at Monster's Lair was how quiet it was. At times when I sat outside in the herb garden, catching the afternoon breeze, I could hear blood droning through my head, my heart tapping out a rhythm. I worried that it wasn't normal, that maybe I was never really relaxed, though I thought I was. Life at Monster's Lair had me grinding my teeth, waking myself in the middle of the night. Hearing the blood pumping in your head didn't seem normal or healthy. Then I realized it was the quiet, quiet like somebody killed it. I could hear my pulse anytime I sat down and listened for it. That was just the way it was.

A wet blanket of silence.

No birds or bugs.

Nothing.

Then Manuel explained it to me.

"You don't hear the birds because of the poison."

"Poison?"

"Monster has the grounds sprayed twice a week with strong insecticide. Yes, they come and spray the lawns and the trees."

"Why?"

"He's allergic to fleas and mosquitoes and spiders. That's what I was told."

"Allergic? You'd think he'd get over it living in the middle of nowhere. That's what's out here, animals and insects. It's wilderness once you get off of the property."

I thought about that as soon as I said it. You had to go some ways to actually get off Monster's property, and you couldn't be sure you were until you reached the on-ramp to the 101. Maybe Monster had his own manifest destiny thing going on and intended to own all of Santa Ynez and spray enough insecticide to debug half the Santa Ynez Valley.

Manuel shrugged and turned away.

"I would consider another job if I could find one that paid like this one. Working here is stress-producing. Too much stress-producing is not good for you," he said.

I remembered that conversation when I heard of Manuel's arrest on suspicion of murder. My cell phone stopped working after we discovered the dead boy. It was odd, really. The few workers I asked said the same thing had happened to theirs; cell phones couldn't find a signal until they were off of the mountain.

Then, once off of the mountain, miraculously the phones worked like they used to. We needed those cell phones because the rooms had no phone lines; the only place to make a call was at the mansion. I was sure my calls were being monitored. Everyone blamed it on Monster because he had the money and the inclination to do something like that.

Monster was an insidious fucker doing his best to overwhelm everyone within his reach, entwine us in a web of confusion and intimidation. What made it embarrassing was that we were being beat down by a caricature of a villain, a gaunt, pale, Saturday-morning-cartoon ghoul.

That's the genius of unbridled wealth, of unlimited resources.

You punk the world.

Since Manuel's arrest, Security tightened their grasp. Those sexless, colorless rent-a-cops constantly patrolled the grounds, watching over everything and everyone with inspired intensity, searching for suspects and suspected informants to the media.

A MEMO, DIRECT AND TO THE POINT, arrived in our mailboxes:

> *Be advised that all contact with media will violate confidentiality agreements. All violations will result in immediate termination and the most vigorous legal action.*
>
> *—Mr. Franzen*

I didn't know a damn thing about anything.

I didn't know this Mr. Franzen; though he seemed to run the administrative staff of Monster's Lair, I had never met him, and no one else I knew had either. Franzen was one more layer between the man we worked for and the gross and teeming world that wanted to get at him, burst through that bubble of mystery surrounding him—and find what? Did they smell encroaching tragedy, a wounded animal that would defend itself with all its remaining strength?

THE MORE I LEARNED of Monster's Lair, the more I realized I didn't know a damn thing; maybe a little more than nothing, but not enough to scribble onto the back of a postcard.

Monster's Lair was a hermetically sealed environment; little got in, and nothing slipped out.

Paid-for silence, deafness, blindness, discretion—silent because there is hardly anyone to talk to, deaf because there is nothing to hear, blind because I don't want to see. So the hunt was on to bring Monster down. I didn't know if he'd done it, overdosed the child, or if it was an accident. One thing I was sure of: Manny wasn't a child killer. That was just obvious bullshit. He had been set up. Unfortunately, I was his alibi, and to tell the truth, that couldn't have done him much good.

On the way to the kitchen I saw police in bright-yellow Windbreakers taking cardboard boxes out of Manny's shed, where he kept his tools and things. You would have thought that he owned every pornographic magazine ever published. Stacks of them covered every inch of the gravel path in front of the shed. I leaned over across the yellow tape to get a better look. Many of the magazines had titles like *TART* or *Young and Fine*. I shook my head. I was sure Manny was being railroaded, but what did I really know?

From a hard sleep I awoke to the sound of someone knocking lightly at the door.

I refused to respond; instead I searched for the cleaver I'd brought from the kitchen.

"Gibson, it's me!" a woman said, urgently.

I didn't know the voice, though I felt I should.

"It's Rita," she uttered in a harsh whisper.

Confused, I knocked the chair aside to open the door. Backlit by the bright lights, Rita stood there, arms wrapped about herself.

I pulled her inside. Tears dampened her face as she silently cried.

"You talk?"

She ignored me and continued to cry, but I needed this miracle, or revelation, or whatever it was explained. The sound of her voice was much heavier than I thought it would be; I'd imagined it would be sweet and ethereal, as sheer as the white nightgown she wore, not husky like a smoker's.

I don't expect miracles in my life, and this wasn't a miracle, though it was a miracle of sorts that she had bullshitted all those months she spent teaching me sign language on that bench in the garden and I had bought it.

I thought she had no voice, but she had just chosen not to use it.

"Rita?"

She looked up at me, and I could see that she verged on hysterics.

"I gave the baby up! Monster has my baby. I let him buy my baby."

Thug was right. Rita was as bought and sold as the rest of us on this strange plantation that grew nothing but grief.

Suddenly, as if under the influence of a tranquilizer, she

calmed down. I helped her to the bed, and then I returned to my chair to sit and think my way through this.

Another knock at the door.

Rita stirred; worried that she might awaken, I quickly opened it.

Thug.

"So, how is she?" he asked with his shit-eating grin.

I wanted to hit him in the face with all the strength I had.

"You want her for the night? It's up to you. Since I know you got a little thing for this girly girl."

I shook my head, confused.

One of Thug's massive hands patted me on the shoulder.

"This is what you want, so don't lie. If you got any designs, you better act on them now. If you don't, I'll carry her back with me."

"She's not some fucking luggage," I blurted angrily, but that just made him laugh.

"No, she's pretty fucking heavy to lug all the way back to the mansion. That's why I'd just as soon leave her here with your ass."

I heard this eardrum-shattering cry from behind me.

Rita sat upright in bed, hands over her mouth, wild at the sight of Thug.

I rushed to the bed to calm her, but almost as soon as I did she drifted back into unconsciousness.

"The drugs, man, are fucking good," Thug said, and

stepped into the bungalow and reached into his pocket and handed me a container of blue striped pills.

"When she wakes up, she'll want these. Give her two and she'll be good. I'll be back in the morning."

I nodded, not knowing what else to say.

"You cool with this, right?"

"Yeah," I mumbled.

"Monster appreciates your help."

I ignored that, though it did give me some sense of relief and spontaneous self-loathing.

"He wants to invite you up to the mansion to sound you out."

"Sound me out? What the fuck does that mean?"

Thug must have enjoyed pissing me off because he laughed very hard.

"Tell you the truth I don't know what that means. He just says things like that and I repeat them, but I bet it's good."

I turned away to shut the door, but Thug's big hand grabbed it.

"Listen, don't get all high on your horse. It's about opportunity. Monster can give you that. You want the cash to start over, have another restaurant? It's all good with Monster. Ain't that what's it about, opportunity?"

"What's this she's said about losing her baby to Monster?"

"What, black? You got to expect that. When you pay top dollar, you want the goods delivered. Right? It's only fair."

I shut the door, this time pulling it hard enough that if he wanted his fingers, he'd get them out of the way.

"Go for what you know, bro" was the last thing I heard Thug say before the door slammed shut.

"Gibson? Come here, I need you near me."

Rita, awake again, tried to swing her legs to the edge of the bed, but she twisted herself up in the sheets and fell to the floor. I hurried to lift her up onto the bed, but before I could retreat, she wrapped her arms around my neck.

"Rita, I don't understand any of this. I don't understand and I need to understand. You have to help me."

She sighed and slipped down in the bed, cover pulled high.

"What do you want to know? I can't explain it. With him I don't have a choice. He's always had me. That's the way it is."

"Why can't you explain it? Why the sign language bullshit?"

She shrugged. "You want to know? After we were married, Monster said he didn't like the sound of my voice, it annoyed him. He didn't ask me to stop talking, but I did. I wanted to stay with him, I wanted what he had to offer me, and so I stopped talking. I tried writing notes, but I realized he wasn't really reading them. He'd just leave them around unopened. He hired a woman to teach me to sign, but he didn't bother to learn it."

"Why did you put up with that? Nobody can do that to you."

"I had no choice."

"You had a choice."

Rita mumbled something and pulled the covers high over her head.

I ripped the covers away.

"What did you say?"

Her eyes flashed.

"You had a choice with cocaine. Did you stop?"

"I was an addict."

"But you could have stopped. You said it ruined your marriage, cost you your career. You had options, what did you do?"

"You know what I did."

"See, don't be hypocritical. I'm weak. I admit that. You're weak too."

She reached for my hand and squeezed it and looked at me for a long minute. Then she reached behind her head to untie the knot to free her nightgown. Her fingers fumbled but couldn't undo the knot.

"Help me," she said. "Don't you want to?"

"Yes," I managed to say, and pointed in the direction of the mansion. "How do you know Monster's not watching?"

She laughed. "I hope Monster is watching. I want him to watch."

"Oh, shit," I said. "I don't want that."

"I'm joking," she replied. "You worry too much."

The nightgown fell.

"Rub my shoulders," she said, stretching out onto the bed.

I started, but my hands quickly found her perfect breasts. I wanted to drink her up, to taste and touch every inch of her, not to go up for air.

I couldn't wait to slip inside, to feel her heat around me. I hadn't been with a woman in so long, I could barely hold back.

But before it happened, right on the precipice of coming, I lost it. I didn't know a damn thing about Rita except that she was crazy, crazy like everyone else here at Monster's Lair.

"Why'd you stop?"

I sat at the edge of the bed, nuts aching, trying to bring myself to ask a question that would make me sound like a total shithead.

"Why did Monster send you here?"

Rita turned onto her side, ignoring me, but I couldn't ignore the curve of her hips, the smoothness of her back.

"Monster didn't send me here, I walked out on him. Thug followed me to make sure I didn't do something stupid. But you don't believe me. You think I'm a liar."

"I don't think you're anything."

"You're being mean. Don't be mean to me."

I had to laugh. I did want to trust her, at least at that moment of suspended lust.

"It's over for me with Monster, he doesn't love me, he never loved me. He wanted me to have his baby. You know he never touched me. He said he doesn't believe in sex."

I raised an eyebrow but tried to keep my mouth shut.

"Did you believe him?"

"I wanted to. I truly did want to believe him because I wanted what he offered."

"What? What was that?"

She shook her head.

"You know I'm not going to tell you. Why do you want numbers? It makes me feel like a prostitute, and you know how Monster feels about numbers."

"I won't ask you again."

"Oh, you don't know how embarrassing it was, having a stupid nurse inseminate me, with Monster too busy in the recording studio to be there. It was all just another lie. Then, when my baby was born, I looked at him and he doesn't look a bit like Monster. He's a blond and blue-eyed, Nordic-looking baby. I'm not a natural blond, as you probably noticed."

She ran her hand between her legs, stroking black pubic hair.

"My family is Sicilian. And whatever Monster is, it's not his baby at all. Could you believe that, that he'd pay for sperm from someone else to impregnate me? And now he wants me to leave so he can have the baby all to himself."

"You have as much right to that baby as he does; more so, since it's not his."

She laughed. "Monster has lawyers, too many lawyers,

just waiting to sue somebody. Me, he'd just lock away in a mental institution."

Her face fell. Tears clouded her eyes, and she returned to her hiding place beneath the covers.

I had decided not to give her the pills; I didn't want to be part of that. But now that she was breaking down, I didn't know. Watching the color wash away from her face, her nervous shaking, low moaning, I didn't want to be responsible.

"I need my medication!" she said, in a voice strained with need.

"What's wrong with you? What are you on?"

"Give it to me, don't make me beg!"

"Here," I said, and handed her one of the four pills.

"I need them all," she said.

"No, what if you overdose?"

"If I had enough, I would."

"What is this shit?"

I looked at the bottle, trying to decipher what Monster had given her.

"Gibson, do you know what Monster is?"

"What do you mean, what he is?"

"You know."

"What, that he's black? That's what he is, no matter how much he bleaches the color out of his skin."

"I'm not talking about that. I know what Monster believes about race."

"You do? I don't know if I care. It's probably as crazy as he is."

"When he started out, he was black, but he changed. He became something else. He says he doesn't believe in race. Do you?" she asked eagerly.

It pained me to see her so fucked up. She was so gone, I wanted to humor her.

"It doesn't matter what I believe about race."

"Monster isn't like you," Rita replied.

I laughed. "That's good, I can live with that."

"Monster did something to himself before I met him. It's worse now. That's another reason he wants me to leave. He doesn't want anyone to see what he's doing to himself."

Listening so hard to her, I didn't notice the pills next to my leg on the bed disappear into her hand and then into her mouth.

"Hey," I said, and tried to reach to take the pills, but she bit my hand, hard.

"Sorry," she said as I rubbed my fingers.

"What are they?" I demanded.

"They keep me from getting hysterical. Monster can't stand for me to get hysterical. I end up writing him a blizzard of notes that he just balls up and throws into the trash."

"Don't you ever just shout at him, call him an ass, and be done with it?"

She shook her head and smiled. "No, that wouldn't work.

When I'm with him, I don't have words. No, not at all."

"Why? I still don't understand how you could stand to be with him under those kinds of conditions."

She laughed, running her hands through her hair.

"I don't know. Really, I don't. You know, you should come back to the mansion with me. Maybe you could talk sense to Monster, make him see what he's doing to himself."

"I don't care about Monster; I care about what happens to you. I don't give a shit about Monster."

"You'll think of something to help him. Make him see how he's hurting himself and me," she said and, as if she was satisfied with her reasoning, she relaxed and leaned back into the bed, pulling me down on top of her. Her breasts felt good, and I moaned when she locked her legs around me and pushed me deeper in. Whatever she was on didn't stop her from making love like she meant it. It didn't leave me with a good feeling, knowing that she was as loaded as she was. Afterward, she fell into a hard, drug-induced sleep.

I put on my pants and stepped outside into the cool night to think.

"You must have liked that. She made you holler," Thug said, silhouetted by brutal security lights. Perfectly comfortable admitting to overhearing our lovemaking, Thug hummed to himself as he leaned jauntily against the bungalow.

"You were listening?"

"Yeah, wouldn't you?"

"No," I said. "I don't do that kind of shit."

"Be a down brother and don't be hating 'cause you got issues."

"I don't have issues with you, I just don't think it's cool to do shit like that."

"I don't have a problem with it. I like listening to people fucking."

Sick of talking to him, I turned to go back inside.

"She's got to come home now," Thug said.

"Why don't you let her stay with me? I can take care of her."

Thug laughed heartily.

"Gibson, man, don't get silly. It ain't smart. Homechick got serious white-girl issues, thinks the world owes her something, and she wants what she wants even if ain't no way in hell she getting that. Then you know she feels like a bitch who got taken advantage of, and she wants revenge. I know you know how deep that is."

"I think I can help her."

"You already helped her and me. She's sleeping so she must have taken her medication."

Thug walked into the bungalow and came back with Rita slung over his shoulder.

"So, dog, tomorrow is your big day. You gonna be kicking it with Monster, eating that fucking uncooked food."

"I cook for him, I don't have time to eat with him."

Monster moved Rita to his other shoulder effortlessly, as though she were a ten-pound sack of potatoes.

"Naw, homeslice. Monster has another cook. He's got something new lined up for you. You out of the cooking game."

Thug rolled up the window and the car raced away. I watched it for a while until I couldn't make out the headlights through the grove of eucalyptus trees. Maybe I couldn't have stopped him, but I could have tried, made a fuss about it, something.

I never thought of myself as being that much of a coward, until that moment.

But I was.

I DIDN'T SLEEP the rest of the night. I wanted a drink, but I fought that desire down and settled for black tea loaded up with sugar, and sat by the kitchen window and watched the sun crawl above the mountains. I didn't deserve to see a beautiful sunrise because I was a contemptible piece of shit.

Monster could corrupt you by having you cook his meals, even something as uncomplicated as serving him dinner. Suddenly, you're implicated, part of the story arc, the narrative of his insanity. I didn't want to be in this story, but I was.

Covered in his filth, I didn't see any way out other than

submerging myself totally in it. Maybe somehow I'd come out on the other end of the cesspool alive. And to believe that I'd survive, I had to have faith. I didn't have that kind of faith. If I had faith, I'd go right to the mansion and demand Monster explain what he was doing to his wife: speak truth to power. Or, if I wasn't capable of something that required courage, I should embrace being a coward and grab my belongings and head off this mountain back to civilization and away from Monster's influence. Rita wasn't totally crazy. I could feel myself being pulled under. It wasn't just her; I too was susceptible. Monster, gigantic in his influence, warped everything around him, and once in his orbit, you hopelessly spun down and down to crash.

Like cocaine, like heroin, like meth.

Weird, to think that Monster had somehow become my new drug and I was dependent on him as much as on any drug I had used. I wanted to be in his world, his sphere of influence, as though his superstar status was shared with me, would rub off on me, when in truth that was bullshit.

IN THE MORNING, I arrived at the kitchen and was surprised to see a turbaned man, all in white, expertly chopping vegetables.

"I didn't know I was sharing my kitchen," I said testily.

The tall, olive-skinned, bearded man smiled in spite of my challenge.

"Hello, pleased to meet you. I am Singh Kupuy," he said in accented English.

"So, you're the new head chef?"

Singh nodded.

"I'm Gibson, the old head chef. I was told I'd be leaving the kitchen, but I didn't think that they would find a replacement so quickly."

Singh's smile vanished.

"You didn't know that I was coming? They hired me over two months ago."

"No, but it's not your fault. Working here is confusing. You never know exactly what's going on."

"That's unfortunate," he said, with genuine feeling.

"Yes, but it keeps things interesting," I added and turned to leave. Then I remembered my set of knives. I didn't want to leave them. I started gathering the knives, and for a moment I worried that Singh might think I was maliciously disappearing things to make his new job more difficult, but I misjudged him.

"Those are very nice. Most of what I see here needs to be replaced."

I laughed. "Yeah, I guess even me."

"I am surprised. You were talked about with great respect. Particularly from Mr. Thug."

"He would, that Mr. Thug is very surprising. But don't worry about me. I'm ready to move on."

"I ate at your restaurant in New York, a few years ago. Very early dinner, I met your beautiful wife, she seated me, and you came over to greet me."

"Really? I forgot that. What did you think?" I asked.

"I liked it very much. You had many good vegetarian dishes."

"I can't take credit for that. My wife oversaw the vegetarian courses."

"Well, the dishes were very enjoyable. I'm trying to bring some of your approach to spiritual eating to Monster's table."

"That's commendable. Monster is an interesting person to cook for."

"How did you come to work here?"

"Bad personal decisions. I'd go into it, but we don't have enough hours in the day."

I grabbed up my knives and turned to leave.

"Good luck, my friend," Singh said.

"Thank you, I need all the good luck I can get. And good luck to you too. I suspect you'll need it."

SECURITY CAME THAT EVENING as I fitfully dozed in an uncomfortable chair. I heard them on the creaky wooden steps and swung the door open so quickly that I startled the two of them. One stumbled backward; the other shone a bright light into my face. They relaxed when they could see I didn't have a butcher knife in my hand.

"Monster wants to see you," the one with the flashlight said.

I glanced from one to the other. They did have physical differences; one's hair was a bit longer than a crew cut. Mostly Security was cut from the same cloth: tall and well built, white and fair-haired.

I shrugged. "I'm ready."

"Turn around," the one with the flashlight said.

"You turn around," I answered.

"This is procedure, to blindfold and handcuff visitors."

"Fuck you. I'm not going to submit to that."

"It is up to you, but Monster requested that you see him."

Security's voice sounded pretty much as they all did, modulated, without a hint of irritation.

I didn't have a choice if I wanted to find out what plans Monster had for me.

They led me to one of the golf cart things they zipped around Monster's Lair in. I turned and let one of them slip a hood over my face and bind my hands with plastic handcuffs.

"Ready?"

"What do you think?"

The way to Monster's mansion seemed wrong, and much longer than it should have taken.

"Where are you taking me?"

Neither responded.

The air felt different, stale, and we traveled on a smoother road.

"Don't be alarmed. We do this because Monster has had a number of threats on his life," Security said after five minutes had passed. My heart beat like I had snorted a long line of coke. What if Monster turned out to be a cannibal or a zombie? A cook gets skewered, and Monster gets to chew on my liver.

Finally we stopped and one of them helped me off the golf cart and led me to a door where they finally freed my hands and took the hood off my head.

I blinked for a moment until my eyes focused.

I was in a cavernous room, empty of everything but a huge roaring fireplace, and in front of it was Monster gently rocking in a chair, cooing to a snugly wrapped baby nestled in his arms. He looked up and waved to Security.

"Bring Mr. Gibson a chair," he said in his odd, girlish voice.

"I can stand," I said.

Monster ignored me. Security hurried away and returned with a heavy leather thing that would have given me a groin pull to lift. He placed it a discreet distance from Monster and stepped away and stood there with his hands behind his back.

"Wait outside," Monster said flatly.

Security turned on his heel. Monster watched him go and laughed lightly.

"Security is always so serious."

I nodded, not knowing whether to laugh or what.

"So, tell me about yourself, Mr. Gibson. How has life at the Lair been treating you?"

I tried to respond, but suddenly I was caught up in a rage I didn't even know I felt, sitting across from him, a man who wore a fedora and sunglasses indoors; I wanted to shout, accuse him of everything that was wrong with Monster's Lair, that dead boy, and me.

I didn't trust myself to talk at that moment, not sure what would come out of my mouth.

"Relax," he said, in a voice that seemed both gritty and childlike. "I know people get uncomfortable speaking to celebrities, but don't be nervous. Relax, we're family here."

"Family? What happened with that dead boy? He had a family."

Monster bolted upright, his sunglasses flew off, and he burst into a wail, an invitation for the baby to wake and join in the cacophony; tears flowed down Monster's cheeks, amazing in their intensity. To his credit, Monster did his best to calm the infant, singing a jagged lullaby and swaying gently. Finally the baby sighed with exhaustion and was quiet.

A door opened, and a nurse appeared and hurried over to take the baby from Monster's arms.

Once they were gone, Monster put his hands in his pockets and glared, his eyes black holes of malice, his face stained with mascara.

"I don't know what happened to Ronnie. He was my good friend and he died."

"Yeah, I know he died. I saw his body, his blue face."

"I loved Ronnie like a son," he said, defiantly. "I would never do anything to harm him."

"No one's accusing you," I said, throwing oil onto the fire.

Monster leaped up, shouting: "Why did that have to happen? Oh, God!"

He lost it; unencumbered by the baby, he filled the huge room with unrestrained grief. I stood up and tried to think how to comfort him. I extended a hand to touch his shoulder, but almost immediately Security appeared.

"Step back!"

I dropped my hand, suddenly surrounded by three uniformed men.

They yanked me around and led me to the door the nurse had left through. Again, the hood was pulled over my eyes but, holding both my arms, they didn't bother to handcuff me. Stairs, six flights, twenty steps a flight; at the landing I heard someone unlock a door, the hood was snatched off, and I was pushed inside. The lead Security stepped to me.

"Enjoy your stay. If you need something—" He pointed to the phone. "We'll bring you dinner in an hour. Monster will reschedule his appointment with you at his earliest convenience."

They backed up and shut the door, keeping their eyes on me as though I might bum-rush them.

I turned around to look at my room or cell or whatever it was supposed to be. The decor was that of a nineteenth-century English tearoom with heavy curtains, dizzying wallpaper, and reproduction antique furniture. My four-poster bed looked more threatening than inviting with its grim green quilt and lacy embroidery. When I saw the minibar, I was reluctant to open it, but I did, to see four bottles of Smothers Brothers Merlot and many minibottles of whiskey and rum. I tried to picture myself pouring everything down the drain and consoling myself with peanuts and Diet Cokes, but I don't have that kind of character. Sitting on the edge of the bed, I polished off a few of the little whiskey bottles and wondered what to do next.

Get drunk? Pick up the phone and demand to be released from a very nice prison?

I opened a bottle of wine and poured a glass.

Bad news; it was drinkable. I proceeded to down the whole bottle. After being on the wagon for so long, it didn't take much for me to have a warm glow in the pit of my stomach that unfurled throughout my body. Anger dissipated, and

I lay there on the bed, feeling content to wallow in self-pity. Still, though, I wouldn't let myself succumb totally to wine-induced catatonia. I forced myself up and walked to the far side of the room. I pulled back the curtains and opened the window, which I found to be almost impossible to budge more than a couple inches. I smacked the glass with my palm. It wasn't glass, but some kind of unbreakable plastic.

I was very high up, at least a hundred feet above the ground. I could see the entire green valley from this room.

I had to be in the tower, the highest point of Monster's mansion, but it didn't look nearly so tall from down there on the ground. Then it occurred to me that I wasn't in that tower; this view of the valley didn't look at all familiar; where was the ocean?

I wondered if I would see him crawling down the side of the building, headfirst.

I opened another bottle of wine, wondering if it would be as good as the last, in my almost pleasant incarceration.

WOKE VOMITING; barely managed to reach the bathroom before my stupid fucking idea of having two bottles of wine came up in a colorful torrent. I sat on the floor of the bathroom, trying to stop the spinning, and spun right back above the bowl, hurling out the rest of my guts.

I showered and returned to bed.

*Naked, running through brush, chasing something or being chased. Thunderous noise blaring behind me, I stop sprinting to glance behind me and see a gigantic white bull rolling along, a freight train gaining on me, see flame erupt from nostrils, white froth spilling from its mouth.*

I woke again, vomiting, lunging again for the toilet, but this time it was just a false alarm, nothing but a stomach-churning dry heave.

After another shower I stumbled to the phone to demand food. I had finished the bowl of nuts a while ago. No dial tone. It figured.

I needed coffee, at least a pot. I tried the phone again. Still dead. The door continued to be locked. I hate pretzels but ate a bag anyway. I wondered when Security would come see about me.

I fell asleep wondering that but woke to a low, monotonous booming. I could feel it through my bare feet, vibrating through the walls. When I put my shoes on, I could still feel it.

A scream? I put my ear to the door. I tried the handle. This time it opened and I stepped into the dimly lit hallway without a clue of what to do. The booming reverberated through the hallway, so loud I felt like I was walking through fog. Singing, something like singing. I wanted to go back to my bungalow. I didn't want to be in the Lair even if Monster planned to offer me the world, but I couldn't stop myself. I found a stairwell and began walking down, counting steps: twenty, forty . . . At three hundred I arrived at the bottom.

I reached out and touched the door, felt the booms through the metal and wood, and pushed it open.

Sound slammed me back like a hard shove to the chest, a beast beating me down to my knees, trance music so loud I worried my eardrums would burst.

Strobe lights flashing, I saw boys, half a dozen of them, young, shirtless blond boys in pajama bottoms sitting cross-legged while Monster swirled in white robes like a rubber-limbed Fred Astaire.

I saw Thug too, watching from the edge of the shadows.

I tried to go back the way I came, hoped to find the stairwell and escape back to semi-imprisonment.

No, locked. I slid to the floor in a dark corner and watched Monster take one of the boys by the hand and pull him up.

The boy was still as Monster moved wildly about him. I gasped when Monster ran his hands around the boy's body in darting caresses.

I didn't want to see this, didn't want to be part of what was going on, powerless to stop it.

But I wasn't powerless.

I had the strength to try; what could they do to me that I hadn't done to myself?

I stood up and took a breath, saw Monster slip the boy's

pajamas down around his knees, hands still running about the boy's body.

"No!" I said, and took a step forward.

My head snapped back and I hit the ground.

"Don't get up. I don't want to beat you down again," I heard Thug say, in this positively friendly voice.

I tasted blood and looked up at the mountain of him.

I braced one trembling leg and tried to get to my feet.

"You are a fool," Thug said, and again a massive fist came from above and connected with the top of my head.

Stars of every color spun in the black void. "Told you to stay the fuck down! You never listen to my advice."

I WOKE UP in the four-poster bed with the green fucking quilt.

I felt like I had the time I fell down a flight of stairs; touched my jaw, as though it ached, but it was fine, not swollen or sore. I shook my head to clear it and tried to stand, but that didn't work very well, and I slipped back to the edge of the bed. Tried to remember last night, but the memory of it was so confusing. I remembered Monster dancing in front of boys, but the rest was hazy, as if my memory had voided itself, like an empty room where you might have left something, but it was gone and it was a waste of time to wait for whatever it was to return.

Then the door opened and Monster came in.

"Mr. Gibson, I came by to see how you were doing," he said in his usual breathless voice.

"I'm fine, just a little tired."

"I heard you had a fall."

"I don't know . . . might have. I don't remember much of what happened last night, had a little too much to drink. Then somehow I seem to have got locked into this room."

"When the kitchen help stopped by to bring you breakfast, they found you on the floor with a knot on your head."

It didn't sound right to me, but it was more of an explanation than I had.

Then Monster pointed to the bottles of wine in the trash can.

"Had a party?"

I shrugged. "I guess so."

"Can we talk?"

I didn't say anything, and Monster sat in the chair across from the bed and crossed his legs. For once he didn't have on his hat or his glasses. Looking at him was fascinating in that his skin was so pale it was almost translucent, and it shimmered. Somehow he'd found a cosmetic that worked like a special effect; when he moved, specks of color lingered in the air.

"I want to apologize. Last night when you mentioned Ronnie, I made quite a scene."

I nodded and looked away so that he wouldn't look at me with those gigantic, empty black eyes.

"My world ain't right up here. Things happen I can't explain. You understand what I'm saying?"

I sat like a stone, waiting for him to continue.

"The police want to talk to you," he said.

"They do?"

"Don't worry. I can have one of my lawyers sit in with you."

"I don't know anything. Why would I need a lawyer?"

Monster stood and looked out of the window with his thin arms folded behind his back.

"It's not just that I have enemies. That happens in life. You make a name for yourself, make some money, and then everybody wants to get up on you."

"Yeah," I said, feeling in my stomach that Monster wanted me to do something for him, something I would not want to do. I could feel it coming.

"I didn't make this place that you see around you. Sure, I added a building or two, restored what needed restoring. I tried to turn it into something that I could love even more. Then the weirdness started happening. Do you know anything about theosophy?"

"No," I said, wondering where he was going with this.

"The dead don't talk to you?"

"No, never," I said, and stepped back.

"People believe different things. I got interested in theosophy a while ago. It makes sense of life for me."

"How?"

"The line between this world and the next isn't as firm as you think."

I wanted to push him out of the room, or the window. What the hell was he saying to me, that a monster from another dimension killed that boy?

"The police don't understand when I try to explain this to them. But they're not aware, they're not enlightened."

I nodded, not having any idea of what he was getting at.

"You're saying a spirit or something killed that boy? He died of an overdose as far as I could see."

Monster turned and looked at me as though he didn't understand a word I said. "I don't know what happened to him, but that's what I'm talking about. I want to have this place exorcised as soon as possible."

"This is off the subject, but I was wondering . . . since you have another chef, I think it's time for me to look for another job. Maybe see if I can convince my wife to take me back."

"That's up to you, but you don't have to. I only let good people work for me, and I know that you are a good person who can be trusted. I take care of my people. You are still on the payroll just as if you're my personal chef."

"Thanks," I said, relieved to know I still had income, but I still felt the other shoe would fall.

"Gibson, I admire your discretion. The situation with my wife is getting worse. We have a beautiful little boy who needs a calm household, and the way things are going here, he's not going to get that with the press digging all around."

He paused and looked at me as though he was trying to read my mind.

"I want you to watch over Rita. Thug isn't very good with her, and no matter how well intentioned his actions are, she gets very upset with him. I value you as a confidant, and I need you to understand what's at stake here. I need you to work with her and keep her on my team. I don't want her to bring this world down on us all."

"I'm willing to do that."

"The sheriff will be at your bungalow at noon."

"I'll talk to him."

Monster smiled winningly at me as he turned to leave. That's what he wanted to hear. Yeah, me the team player. I would be his boy if that's what it took to make things right. I was in.

Security came to escort me back to my bungalow, but this time they didn't bother with the handcuffing and the hood. I rode that golf cart just like Security did because I was now more or less Security, ready to protect Monster at all costs.

I can't say I was happy to step onto the wooden front porch of my bungalow; overjoyed was more like it.

The air in Monster's Lair, deep inside of it, seemed wrong, like it was fouled with something tasteless and odorless. Maybe Monster was right and there was something really wrong with the place, something that didn't involve him, but I doubted it.

I SLEPT HARD THAT NIGHT, without dreaming, but I woke at dawn with a clarity of thought that I hadn't experienced in weeks. With this sudden burst of energy, I decided to go for a run. I changed into shorts and a T-shirt, stretched for a few minutes, and started at a trot. I didn't mean to go far or fast, but once I started, feeling my way through creaks and pain, I didn't want to stop after a mile of running the trails on the outskirts of Monster's Lair. I saw Security checking me out, talking on their cell phones; in the distance the media was there, still camped, and the government vehicles were along the roads, some double-parked.

Where was I?

Running, clearing my head, remembering.

Monster had done something to me. The dryness in my mouth, my heart beating so hard, me feeling so good.

I had been drugged.

Shit happened there, and I could remember only shards of it, memories cracked into pieces too small to reassemble.

Problem was they didn't know what a drug addict knows, a drug addict like me. I had done enough speed, coke, and heroin to know what a buzz is, even one that wasn't intended to get you high.

A psychedelic?

Monster or Thug, somebody should have thought of the obvious truth before trying that acid in the wine: Dope fiends know their dope.

I finished the run and walked slowly back to the bungalow, wondering what Monster had hoped to accomplish.

Maybe he worried that I wouldn't be a team player, and needed insurance that if I did know something I wouldn't be able to speak to it with certainty.

I showered and waited on the porch with a tall glass of ice water, debating whether I should tell the sheriff of my suspicions, though I knew I wouldn't. Then I saw the black-and-white roll up the gravel road. Sheriff Graves wasn't a personable man. When I first came to Santa Ynez, I had to report to the station to register as a parolee. I was surprised to be interviewed by the top lawman in town. And he treated me with contempt, barely speaking to me. I wondered if he disliked me for being a New Yorker. When he asked me to confirm where I had lived and worked, I said New York, and he repeated the word as though New York had syphilis.

Graves walked over to me without looking up, until I thought he might step on my toes.

I stood to greet him, but he sat down next to me.

"Listen, Gibson, I should take you down to the station and get another statement, but I'm short-handed with all these interviews we got to do and can't spare somebody to drive you back."

"Okay," I said, thinking that was fine with me.

"I got a question for you, and I want you to take your time in answering."

"Sure."

His blue eyes were shot through with red. Must not have slept much in days.

"I hope you know what a piece of flying shit this has turned out to be. I'm so sick of these fucking reporters, goddamn cockroaches. And the lawyers are worse than the reporters. Surprised you're willing to talk. His lawyers have everybody clammed up."

I shrugged. "I don't mind talking, but I don't have much to say."

The sheriff's eyes narrowed.

"Let me ask the questions and I'll worry about how much you know."

"I'm fine with that."

Graves stood up and nodded to a van parked by the mansion.

"See that goddamn van? Monster's people are watching. Come on."

He gestured for me to follow him, and we stepped behind the bungalow, which faced open country.

"Those Security yahoos are using a directional mic to listen to us whenever they get the chance. I'm telling you this though I can't prove it, but that's okay. I've complained enough, to the point where I think I'm talking to myself when I talk to them. They deny it all, but I know they hear me."

"So what do you want from me?" I asked.

"Well, hear this, you know you're being set up."

"I am?"

"Sure. Why do you think they're letting you talk to me? They have all of their employees with a lawyer right at their shoulder, making sure everything goes according to plan."

"What plan?"

"For you and the Mexican to be the fall guys, the patsies."

"That's not going to happen. I never trusted Monster."

"That's good because you shouldn't. You should be talking to your lawyer. Off the record, like I've said, you've already been fingered."

"Fingered me? How?"

"How long have you been collecting child porn?"

"I've never collected child porn! I've never seen any child porn," I said, sputtering with anger.

"We searched your bungalow," Graves said, without looking at me.

"How can you do that without my permission or a court order?"

Graves smirked.

"Mr. Stiles gave permission. It is his property."

"But . . ."

He interrupted me with a wave of his hand.

"We didn't find anything, but someone left an anonymous message on my voice mail about you and your relationship to Manuel Flores, that you both are pedophiles."

"Yeah, that's a crock. I don't have any interest in children. I don't even want children of my own. That's just a load of shit for someone to say that about me."

The sheriff looked at me for a long minute. "Maybe I believe you. What about this Manuel Flores? No history of molestation and then we find a mother lode of child porn in his work area. It's kind of pathetic. You'd think they'd do a better job of going about this setup."

"So what do you think I should do?"

"I want you to report to me whatever you see Monster doing."

I nodded, but I wasn't at all sure I wanted to get into it at that level. I wasn't constitutionally suited to narc on anyone.

"I don't trust Monster, but I don't want to get into something I can't handle."

"Suit yourself. Just remember I'm extending an olive

branch to you because I believe you're innocent and getting reamed. Now, I don't want to be left hanging, like those fucking idiot police in that Ramsey case. I want this to end and the media gone."

"Tell you the truth, working here is like being in a strange dream. Most of the time I don't know what the hell is going on moment from moment. It's a constant state of confusion. I think there's something in the air, in the water."

Sheriff Graves laughed.

"Yeah, well, I can't say I like coming out here. First of all, no one says anything without a lawyer. I know Monster has them sign their lives away if they want to work for him. It's useless trying to get anyone to tell the truth. I tried to follow up on allegations of drug use, but Monster's money carries a lot of weight. I can't fight that, and I can't get state money to fund investigations. After a while you get tired of beating your head against a wall, and you just let it go. Some people shouldn't be parents, they should have to apply for a license to be parents, but this is different. A child died and someone is going to pay for that!"

Sheriff Graves slapped the wall with such force I thought he might have broken his hand. He rubbed his palm and stared at me.

"What do you want me to do?"

"Nothing, right now. Just keep your eyes open. They think we'll go after you because Manuel disappeared."

"Manuel disappeared?"

Graves nodded. "We brought him in for questioning. He had some interesting things to say, then we got that tip about you. I didn't bring you in because it seemed too convenient. I mean, you don't have a history of child abuse; you had a drug problem that you're being tested for. You have a parole officer and you're checking in. It didn't add up to me. Manuel disappeared after the investigation turned in your direction."

"I had nothing to do with this, and I'm sure Manuel didn't have anything to do with this."

"How well did you know him?" Graves asked.

I shrugged. "Not well at all."

I didn't want to look him in his eyes because I was afraid I might say what I really felt.

"What do you think happened to Manuel?" I asked.

"From what I hear he went back to Mexico."

"Why would he run?"

"He had some things in his background," Sheriff Graves said.

"Like what?"

"I can't go into that, but I have my doubts that he had anything to do with the kid's death."

Hearing that he didn't suspect Manny was a tremendous relief.

"Tell me something before I go. What's it like in there? I only saw a few rooms," he said, pointing to the mansion.

"It's huge, a maze. I couldn't find my way around inside. I wanted string to unwind behind me."

"Did you see many children in there? He's been stonewalling about that."

Images of boys dancing in Monster's private *Nutcracker* flashed in my mind.

"I saw some, but can't say for sure. My memory is hazy. But I don't get these parents."

Sheriff Graves sighed. "You know the answer, it's money, just money."

"Yeah, I guess so."

"He throws it around, and people are willing to look the other way, even when it comes to their own kids."

"It's amazing someone hasn't shot him."

"Okay, I don't want you shooting anybody. Don't think of doing something involving guns. All you need to do is let me know what's going on. That's it! I don't want you doing anything stupid, playing hero," he said, with a menacing squint. "You understand what I'm saying?"

I nodded. "Yeah, I got it."

"Don't mean to bust your balls on this, but if you get to thinking too hard about Monster, it ain't good. Let me tell you I've had a few daydreams of putting it to him. I mean, the man's a child-molesting black man who bleaches his skin white, and folks accept it because he pays the taxes around here."

"Yeah," I said, glad that Sheriff Graves wasn't too swift on the uptake and hadn't noticed my bleached blackness.

Glancing about, as though he might be spied on, he handed me a pager.

"If you get into serious trouble, use this. Press the orange button and I'll get out here fast as hell."

"You think I'll need it? Monster is going to have me killed or something?"

Sheriff Graves smirked.

"I don't know what that man might be capable of."

I nodded, and he walked back to the patrol car. When he was gone, I looked over the pager; the little nondescript box had a bad feeling to it. If I ever had to push the button, I wondered what kind of nightmare I'd be in.

## KUMQUAT AND HABANERO CHILE JAM

MAKES 1½ CUPS

- 1 large blood orange
- 1 cup sugar
- ½ cup seeded, sliced kumquats
- 1 habanero pepper, seeded and julienned
- 2 tablespoons orange juice (freshly squeezed)

Using a peeler, remove the orange rind and reserve it; then cut off and discard the white pith underneath. Set the orange aside.

Put the rind in a medium saucepan and add cold water to cover it by 1 inch. Bring to a boil; drain. Repeat 2 more times. Let the rind cool slightly.

Finely chop the rind and the reserved orange; put in a medium saucepan and add the sugar, kumquats, habanero, and 2 cups water. Bring to a boil; reduce the heat; and simmer, stirring occasionally, until the water has evaporated, 35 to 45 minutes. Let cool; then mix in orange juice.

# CHAPTER SEVEN

I FIRST SAW THE DOG FROM A DISTANCE, posing on a rise, and thought it was a statue of heroic proportions that Monster had installed earlier that day and that I had only just noticed. I stepped off of the porch into darkness instead of perpetual daylight. The security lights that made Monster's Lair bright as Yankee Stadium were dimmed for some reason. No, the only illumination was the moon, hanging low like a Chinese lantern, bathing the grounds in a bluish glow. I wanted to see, to get a better look at this dog. I walked along the broad pebble path that I knew well, but I almost fell when I saw the huge beast of a dog on the hill before the expanse of lawn in front of the mansion.

The dog tossed its head back and howled, deep and urgent. Then it focused its attention in my direction. My curiosity fled as quickly as I tried to do, running hard to the bungalow. I didn't hear the sound of a massive dog closing on me, but I ran, ran as hard as my lungs could stand, and raced up the steps of the porch and managed to get the door open and my ass inside.

I flung a chair against the door, but I was sure the dog could burst through if it wanted to. I heard nothing and sighed. Whatever poisonous vibe resonated at Monster's Lair, its volume had been ratcheted up.

THE NEXT MORNING I heard a car drive up and the sounds of two people approaching the door of the bungalow, but before they knocked or I got out of bed, the door flew open. The morning light made me squint, but I still could see Thug's huge arm sweep Monster into the room. I sat up to greet them and find out what kind of trouble I was in.

Monster smiled and waved for Thug to leave. He sat on the edge of the bed, wearing black silk pajamas, sunglasses, and a bright-green fedora. He crossed his hands and waited as though he expected me to ask a question.

I didn't say a thing.

"Well, how did your conversation go with Sheriff Graves?" he asked, almost in a whisper.

"We talked. He wanted to know what I knew about what goes on here. I don't know what goes on here so I didn't have much to say."

"Did he ask you anything specifically, anything 'bout the boy?"

"You mean the dead boy?" I said, and watched Monster flinch.

"Yes, that's exactly who I mean," he said, just as softly.

"He asked me about him. I said I never saw the boy before and didn't know how he died, though I suspected he overdosed."

Monster's mouth fell open.

"You told him that?"

"Yes, I did. Anybody who saw that body would have known that the boy had overdosed. That might not have killed him, the overdose, maybe he suffocated somehow. Who knows? I'm not a coroner."

Monster shuddered, and his placid expression gave way to grief. It took a minute for him to compose himself.

"Listen, other than that, I need to discuss another matter with you. I'm not sure how you'll feel about this, but I think it would be good for you, for me . . . and Rita."

"What?" I said, probably too quickly.

Monster straightened his pajama top, ran his hand through his mop of hair (he had an exceptional weave), and focused his concealed gaze onto me.

"Earlier I talked to you about coming on board with me, in a different capacity."

"Yes, I remember."

"Well, this is it. What I need you to do. I want you as a consultant."

"As a consultant? The only thing I know is food, that's my business."

"I need your advice about Rita. She's not doing well."

"I don't know. I think I should find work in my area of expertise."

Monster stood up and reached into a pajama pocket and came out with a checkbook. He started to scribble in such a dramatic, theatrical fashion I thought it would be illegible, but when he handed the check to me, it was very clear. A check for fifty thousand dollars.

"Is that enough for you?"

"What am I supposed to do for this money?"

Monster wrote another check just as dramatically.

He handed that one to me with disdain, as though touching it hurt him.

Another fifty thousand.

"My gifts to you. I want you to take them now and leave, go straight to the bank, and deposit them."

"I don't know what to say."

"You don't have to say anything, the money is yours."

"Thanks," I said uneasily; it didn't feel right taking the money, but I couldn't bring myself to give the checks back.

"Thug!" Monster called, and the big man appeared.

"Drive him to Solvang so he can deposit his checks."

Thug nodded. "I'll get the ride," he said. I stood on the porch, waiting for Thug to return with the car. Monster stayed in my room, and though he had just given me two checks for a total of a hundred grand, I wasn't comfortable with that.

I glanced back, and there he was, sitting on the edge of my bed, as if ready for an early-morning nap. I guessed, for the kind of money he had just dropped on me, I could forgive that, if he didn't use my pillows. I should have been able to stand the idea of that, or him even getting under my sheets. No, I'd have had to get rid of the bedding, burn that shit. To my relief, Monster finally wandered outside, and though it was just a short walk, he produced an umbrella and opened it to shield himself from the soft morning sun.

Thug arrived and hurried to open the door of the Maybach for Monster.

"No, I'll walk back. I want him at the bank when it opens so he can take care of business."

Thug nodded; we waited for Monster to meander up the path back to the Lair before I stepped into the backseat of the massive sedan. Before I could sit comfortably, Thug hit the gas. Gravel spewed in every direction. We started down the steep and narrow road until he slammed on the brakes and I fell forward. Thug stopped to struggle with a stack of CDs. A moment later the sound of Maze's "Happy Feelin's" flooded the cavernous compartment and Thug nodded with contentment. "I love me some Maze," he said, nodding his big head.

Maze made me feel like I had overdosed on Valium; too much happiness for me to keep down. Maybe that's how Thug could survive Monster and even thrive: his appetite and appreciation for the insanely optimistic.

The Pacific Ocean showed itself around one switchback and again when we neared the 101.

I wanted to be at that bank already. Those checks in my pocket were burning against my leg. I couldn't suppress it, the joy I felt. My ship had come in; I'd be able to breath easily and think clearly about my next move. Now that I had got a taste of Monster's money I wanted more, wanted to drink from it, the unlimited fountain of wealth that he wanted to bestow on me. I wanted to swim in it, maybe even drown in it.

I felt Thug's heavy hand on my shoulder.

"Didn't I tell you that Monster is good to his word? When he says he going to do something for you, he don't bullshit."

"I guess so. I never had somebody just give me a hundred thousand."

"You got a guess on how much Monster is worth?"

I shook my head. "I don't have a clue."

"About four hundred million. What he gave you, he wipes his ass on. That muthafucka sneezes a hundred K. See, I'm bringing in about fifty grand a month, plus bonuses. I save that shit too. I don't waste it 'cause I know this ain't gonna last. One day this house will come crashing down around all our heads."

"Why?"

"Somebody is gonna catch on to what goes on here. You know if Monster wasn't paying off everybody, he'd be much richer. Shit, sometimes when I get to adding all them numbers up, it makes me sick to my stomach . . . He's paying, damn, it must be two million a month."

"You think?"

"Look at you. You just got paid. And you gonna keep getting paid. See, me, I keep my eyes closed. I don't want to know what he's doing. When that famous lawyer Tommy Cocktail comes in from Beverly Hills and sets a card table up in front of the gates and the parents bring their boys and sign a release and I escort the boys into the mansion, I turn around and leave. And the boys have a slumber party. The next day when the kids are gone and Monster calls you in to take care of something and on the nightstand you see the Polaroids, the unimaginable, you know everybody gets paid."

"Why you telling me this? I thought this was the kind of shit you were supposed to keep to yourself."

Thug smiled, showing a mouth full of beautiful teeth.

"I'm a muthafucking dog."

"Yeah, well, I know that."

"That's part of the deal when he hired me. I can't help it, it's part of my dog nature. I got to be true to that."

"You got to be," I said, finding myself admiring this giant, psychotic, gay black man.

A COUPLE OF POLICE were drinking coffee outside of a Starbucks, next to the Bank of Solvang. Thug didn't even slow when he turned into the strip mall like he owned the world. Monster did own the strip mall we'd just entered, or so Thug told me when he parked the Maybach. He gave the police the brother man nod, and we headed into the bank.

"All right, dog, you take care your bizness and I'll take care of mine."

I nodded with a lump in my throat. I didn't want to think about the possibility of getting played. I wanted this to work so much it made my head hurt.

The cashier, a cute blonde, took a look at my check and called for the manager.

He came quickly, a short man with bushy eyebrows, and asked for me to sit down.

"You're working out at Monster's Lair?"

"Yes, for about a year."

"Would you like to open an account? Many of Mr. Stiles's employees have accounts here." He handed the checks over to me. "You'll need to endorse these."

As I signed them, I found myself asking a question I didn't know I had been formulating.

"How long will it take for these funds to be available?"

"They're available now. Mr. Stiles has a very special relationship with us, and once we ascertain that the check is legitimate, your monies are available."

"Oh," I said calmly, but I felt light-headed. Giddy even with the idea of cashing out now. Take the money, buy a car, and drive away into the sunset. Be done with Monster and his cast of characters, and see what life has to offer with Elena. Really, it made no sense to stick around, but something held me back. It would be so easy if not for the promise of dipping into that river of endless wealth that ran right through Monster's Lair. It felt like the late nineties, when everybody with sense knew the bubble couldn't last, but folks still threw down into the crap game because if you didn't get in maybe you'd miss out on what was still to be got.

Who knows?

Who knows what Monster might pay to guarantee my silence?

Yeah, it could be astronomic.

That's what I needed. All the money I could scoop up in my hands, in a bucket, a garbage truck, a barge.

Just like anybody who had the opportunity to get paid, I discovered the greedy fuck that I am; I wanted all the money.

It couldn't be a good decision to risk whatever I had accomplished since getting out of prison, the halfway house, and the wreck I had made of my life. Maybe it was curiosity, to see how it would play out, how everything would resolve. What would happen with Monster? What would happen to me?

I tried to make up my mind as I sat there in an uncomfortable, overstuffed chair, watching the bank clerk process paper.

Freedom or money?

Return to Monster's Lair to make my fortune, or take what I had and go?

No reason to lie to myself, no reason to do that at all.

I WALKED TO THE PARKING LOT with ten thousand dollars in my pocket. That was my compromise: bet 10 percent on freedom, 90 percent on getting rich. The beauty of the Central Coast and me disappearing into it seemed past me now, its allure tarnished by the glint of gold.

I was part of Monster's entourage, willing to go for the gold. I stood by the Maybach, waiting for Thug to return, but I didn't see him creep up and hit me in the shoulder with a rolled-up magazine.

"Check it out," he said.

I unfolded it, a real estate throwaway.

"I'm thinking of buying this little winery. Yeah, bet I could make bank with my own Zinfandel. You know brothers like sweet wine. 'Thug's Zinfandel, fine wine for the gangsta!' "

He unlocked the doors, and I slid into the front seat; almost instantly my stomach churned. I tried to rush my head out of the window, but a half second too late, and I vomited against the door.

Thug scowled in my direction. "Damn, nigga. You sick? Now I gotta get this fucking car washed."

Before I could apologize, my stomach erupted all over again.

This time I managed to vomit mostly out of the window, but that didn't please Thug much.

"What the fuck did you eat? Next time put your head out of the window!"

I listened to Thug yell as my head swirled in waves of queasiness.

I should have regarded my stomach as some kind of gastric early-warning system and leaped out of the car soon as Thug slowed at a light, but no, I didn't have that kind of common sense.

Thug dropped me off in front of my bungalow, still seething at me, though I paid for the car wash. He barely slowed long enough for me to get out.

Then he slammed on the brakes and called to me.

"Monster wants you at a dinner party at six."

I nodded, annoyed, but I had to admit I was curious about what that Sikh chef was making for Monster.

THE LAIR WAS LIT as it was for parties; instead of blazing white light directed out to blind, purple and gold beams of illumination colored the spires and turrets of the mansion's faux-Gothic facade. It looked almost inviting, warm and even comfortable, if you could believe that. I walked across the drawbridge with a sense of foreboding and curiosity, armed with a bottle of Pepto-Bismol in my pocket.

Security stopped me at the giant doors of the mansion and waved a metal detector about, then patted me down. One of them noticed the Pepto-Bismol and gave it close scrutiny.

"What's this?"

"Take a look," I said. "It's for my stomach."

"Take a drink," the guard said while the other Security positioned himself behind me.

I took a couple of sips and put the top back on the bottle. They waited for me to swallow.

"See, it's not poison," I said, wiping the pink from my lips with the back of my hand.

Security didn't crack a smile.

"Go on in," he said.

It was the first time I'd ever stepped into Monster's Lair through the front, having always used the servants' door. Monster, or his interior decorator, had the taste of somebody who liked the clutter of pretentious hotel lobbies and had a fetish for Art Deco. I wasn't surprised to see a coat of arms prominently displayed above the fireplace, as if Monster was descended from a long line of European nobility instead of being from a project in Houston. By the fire, I saw a small party of dinner guests seated in chairs so large they were lost in them. I stepped down into this great hall that couldn't under any circumstances be considered intimate. Even in the dim light of the fireplace I recognized the tall and disturbingly thin figure of Monster, who waved and hurried over to greet me. He took my hand into his thin, reedlike one and vigorously shook it.

"So glad you could make it. I really need you on my team."

"Yes," I said, trying to appear enthusiastic when in fact being in the presence of Monster was alarming enough to make me pat around for my bottle of Pepto-Bismol.

"Come and join the party. I think you know most of the guests."

Still holding my hand, Monster led me over to them. He was right, I did know the guests, and I was very surprised to see them: Asha and Bridget were huddled on the couch like cornered animals. I waved to Asha and wanted to talk to her, but she wouldn't look in my direction. She didn't look like a woman who was happy to be at a party, or to be seated next to a boy. I guess I shouldn't have been surprised to see another of those ubiquitous blond boys, but Monster was so blatant about it. That boy looked up at Monster with utter adoration.

With a regal gesture, Monster gestured for everyone to stand.

"Dinner is ready," he said, and we followed him to another cavern of pretentious dimensions with a chandelier so large that it occupied most of the broad ceiling. Monster directed us to a magnificent flower-strewn table, large enough to seat a football team but that in comparison to all the ostentation around it was inviting and tasteful.

"Please, sit down."

Monster pointed to a chair next to the boy, but I politely ignored him and sat next to Asha. "How are you?" I whispered to her.

"I'll talk to you later," she said, barely moving her lips.

A waiter appeared with the first course. I guess I should have been stunned at such a complete reversal of Monster's eating habits, but for whatever reason I wasn't. Small azure bowls filled with beef tartar were placed in front of us.

I lifted up the bowl and smelled thyme and garlic.

I glanced up and saw Asha looking at the meat with barely concealed disgust.

After the busboy cleared away the azure bowls, the waiter returned with a tray of small red bowls filled with ceviche marinated with lemon and basil and laced with slivers of various hot peppers.

Monster still was doing the uncooked thing, but obviously had given up on the vegetables.

Monster and his companion seemed to be heartily enjoying themselves as they tasted from each other's bowls. When the veal carpaccio was served, Asha quickly left the table. Monster didn't seem to notice, so I followed her outside to the pool, which stretched to the horizon and disappeared like a waterfall onto the world below.

Asha finally looked at me.

"I can't believe you served me raw meat," she said, with disgust.

"I didn't serve you, and I don't cook for Monster. He gave that job to another chef. I do something else for him. I don't know exactly what it is, but it pays a lot better."

"Yeah, that's how it is with Bridget too. You're on the payroll and that's all that matters."

"What do you mean?"

"It's too complicated and fucked up to go into. Suffice it to say that Bridget can't quit, and I've got to be a team player. Bridget wants me to follow her lead to humor this man. I guess that's how it is, we've got to humor the rich, especially when it comes to eating. What happened to him? Last I heard, he was some sort of super-vegan. Did you get him on this meat kick?"

I shook my head. "You need to ask his current cook."

A warm wind blew, and the beaded curtain separating the dining area outside from the kitchen entrance rustled. I took some of the beads into my hand and looked out toward the northeast.

"The wind is so warm," Asha said.

"It's those Santa Anas," I said, having just read that winds from the east were the Santa Anas.

"Is that fire?" Asha asked, pointing to a touch of red at the edge of the blackness.

"I think so," I said. "This is the time of year when brush-fires get out of hand."

Asha scowled. "I wish this fucking place would just burn down. Look at all of us here, indulging this disgusting man. I know he's poisoned us all, I can taste it . . . I see the little flashes of color flickering on the edge of my vision, we're hallucinating. I hope this place burns to the ground."

"I want that too, matter of fact. Being bought gives you all kinds of rage."

"Yes, well, I've always wanted to start a woman's shelter, I've just never had the funding. I have it now, from an unknown benefactor."

"Monster?"

"Yeah, he didn't stay unknown very long. Everybody is in his web of influence."

"How do you feel about that?" I asked, already knowing the answer.

"I hate it. I feel like I've been corrupted, and while I don't have many illusions about myself, I never thought I'd sink this low."

"Welcome to the club," I said. "But I've come to accept it, you know, that working for Monster makes me feel like I'm covered in shit."

"Oh, yes. I know exactly what you mean, but at this point, between Bridget and me, we don't have many good options."

"With Monster, somehow it seems there are no options but to take the money."

"Is that how it is with you? Your parole is up; you could get on with your life. Why the hell are you here?"

At first I tried to come up with something that sounded better than the truth, but that was impossible.

"For the money. I can't think of a better reason than that."

"Glad you're honest because you can't lie to me. I'm a trained social worker."

"Yeah, I remember that," I said with a smile.

"How easy it is to get involved in something so wrong, and then try to find all the reasons in the world to justify it."

We walked back in time for dessert: chocolate pudding in enormous cups with fresh whipped cream, more delicious than any pudding had a right to be. But I lost my appetite when I saw Monster spoon-feeding his friend. Monster leaned over to wipe some chocolate from the boy's cheek and slyly kissed him.

We all saw it, but we acted as if it was nothing to see. The kiss went on for an agonizingly long moment.

I guess I shouldn't have been surprised when Bridget began to silently sob, her cries suppressed but still shaking her. Asha led her out, and I sat there alone with Monster and the boy.

Monster obviously wanted us to be involved in his debauchery as passive participants, as witnesses. He rubbed the boy's shoulders, and then his hand slipped lower, almost to his crotch.

I got up to leave. I didn't want to see this, even if I couldn't do anything about it, even if I was paid not to do anything about it.

"Gibson, sit," Monster said without looking in my direction. I continued to stand.

"I want to explain myself to you," he said.

After a moment, I realized that he wanted my permission.

"You don't need to explain yourself to me."

"But I want to," he said as he gave the boy a pat on the ass and sent him on his way.

Alone, he took off his dark glasses and waved his hands like he intended to communicate with sign language, but then I realized he had made the sign of the cross.

"Before we get started, I hope you remember how I told you that I suspected that this place isn't right? Well, I brought in someone to perform a cleansing. He gave me this."

Monster held up a delicate glass atomizer.

"Mr. Chow is one of the foremost spiritualists in the world today. He has developed a plan to cleanse the estate, and I believe in his plan," Monster said with so much conviction that he must not have been completely sold on the talents of Mr. Chow and needed to finish convincing himself.

Monster sat at the edge of the couch and again made odd gestures with his hands.

"I can feel the changes in the energy around here. Do you feel it?"

I nodded.

"How is it for you? Do you see it? Sometimes I see the colors and auras. Do you see them?"

"I don't think it works too well for me," I said, hoping that Monster would get bored with my lack of enthusiasm about whatever he was getting at.

"Yesterday Mr. Chow burned sage in each room, but he asked me to use this often to dispel negative energies."

I should have seen it coming; maybe I could have held my breath, or turned and run. He reached for a gold atomizer and squeezed the rubber bulb, and I got a faceful of what tasted like rose water.

Instantly, I was high. I've used many drugs, many times, and yet I had never experienced anything so fast and powerful. Monster's words flowed together so quickly I couldn't pull them apart. I did see colors, dark, low purples that reverberated right out of my grasp.

I was very high, speeding gently on my way to whatever level of consciousness Monster was at.

"The wind and the fire are a manifestation of the negative energy around us. You agree?"

I couldn't answer since I was panicked into silence over the idea that he had poisoned me again with whatever he had drugged me with the first time.

"But since Mr. Chow has been here I feel the current is changing. I feel more positive."

"That's important," I managed to say.

"I do need your help in one area we had discussed."

"What do you need me to do?"

"Rita still doesn't understand that my feelings for her have changed. She can't accept that. I've tried to get her to listen to reason, but it's not working. If you could get her to think about what's best for the baby, I'd be very grateful. She's not a good parent. She can't see that. You see that, don't you?"

I nodded.

"It's hard to be a good parent. It might be a gift. I have it and she doesn't."

He didn't blink as he stared at me, waiting for a word to slip from my lips. I tried to organize my thoughts. Was I ready to say anything to get paid?

"Will you help me?"

"What do you want me to do?"

Monster smiled with relief at my answer. "She needs to leave. She needs to find herself a life. I've given her enough money to go wherever she chooses, but she wants to stay here. I can't have that. Maybe you can reach her."

Again I saw the sparks around Monster. If he lifted a hand or moved his head, little bursts of color trailed about him. It had to be that spray—was it acid? I hadn't had acid since college, and I didn't remember acid working so completely or so quickly.

Monster laughed and a cascade of twinkling lights radiated about him.

I reached to touch one, and Security, always omnipresent, appeared.

Monster waved them away.

"I need to go. I'm not feeling so well," I said.

Monster giggled.

I wanted to laugh, but I couldn't. I wanted to be angry that he'd got me high again, wanted me to do his dirty work, do something with his wife, take her off his hands so he could have the baby to himself.

"Monster, do you ever think you might be wrong about the things you do?" I asked, watching the words tumble out of my mouth.

Soon as I had asked the question, I wished I hadn't. It wasn't a good question, and I didn't want to know the answer. Whatever reason I was there, it wasn't to get thrown out on my ass just when I was in good with him. But Monster didn't take offense. Instead, he thought for a minute; then, as if satisfied with what he had come up with, he answered me.

"No, never. I do what God wants me to do. I'm a servant of the righteous and divine."

"Right on," I said, and left. On my way back to the bungalow a fragment of a song floated up to me, hanging words, faintly glowing in the dark: "If there's a hell below, we're all gonna go."

## ALMOND BUTTERSCHNAPPS CARAMEL

*Note: This recipe was specifically formulated for metric measurements, so you will need a kitchen scale that shows grams. You will also need a candy thermometer in degrees Celsius.*

680 grams sugar
680 grams evaporated milk
1 vanilla bean
250 grams cream
570 grams glucose syrup
40 grams butter
95 grams "butterschnapps" (butterscotch) liqueur
25 grams salt
400 grams almonds, toasted

In a pot, cook the sugar, evaporated milk, vanilla bean, and cream to 110°C. Then add the glucose and butter. Cook again, this time to 115°C. Remove the pot from the heat and stir in the butterschnapps, salt, and nuts.

Pour into prepared candy molds or into a pan lined with parchment paper. Let the candy cool completely before removing it from the molds or cutting it into pieces.

# CHAPTER EIGHT

THE NEXT DAY THE FIRE BURNED CLOSER to the 101 and toward Solvang, but the winds had changed and the ash had vanished. Still, I wanted to stay in my bungalow and not bother going out into the soot-filled morning. I needed to check on Rita as Monster had asked, though I also wanted to see Rita because I wanted to. I had avoided it, suspecting that an explosion would follow. She'd discover what kind of shithead I am, that I was a tool for Monster. I've never been the kind of man who could sleep with a woman and not feel connected to her. No, I think I'm genetically predisposed to monogamy. I felt that connection to Rita, but nothing good could come out of it because I was on Monster's team, and I'd soon enough be returning to Elena.

I walked up the stairs that led to the private pool that faced the southwest corner of the Lair. I found her on a towel, tanning. I was reminded of just how beautiful she was naked. I thought of how lucky I was to have made love to her, even if she was nuts. Yes, at that moment her being crazy didn't matter at all; I'd do it all over again. Then, coming out of the pool, pulling himself up with massive arms—Thug. He too was naked, and it suited him as much as Rita. Seeing Thug glistening in the morning sun, naked and of superhuman proportions, I felt so totally outclassed that I wondered if I was of the same gender.

"Gibson, get your ass in the pool. Once the wind changes, you might never get the chance again. I'm betting this place is gonna burn to the ground."

I shook my head. No way would I be taking off my clothes anywhere near him. I didn't need that kind of humiliation.

Thug poured himself a glass of champagne from the bottle in the ice bucket at the table under the umbrella. Maybe Thug was psychic; the wind changed, and almost immediately I saw drifting ash.

Rita turned over and looked toward me, but I nervously averted my eyes.

"So, I heard Monster wants you to talk to me."

"Monster told you that?" I asked as I squatted down next to her, my hand shielding my eyes from the sun, and from the sight of Thug's prodigious manhood. Thankfully, he put a towel over his lap, freeing me from twisting my neck so as not to look in that direction.

"No, Monster didn't tell me that. Thug told me."

Thug sat up and nodded.

"He also told me what he wants you to do. Your job is to get me to leave. You're supposed to help me to forget about my baby."

"Thug told you all that?"

"Yeah," Rita said, nodding at Thug.

"How much did he offer you to do that, dog?" Thug asked.

"He didn't. I didn't say I would do anything other than talk to Rita, which I'm doing now."

"Still, man, you should have got something up front. Cash, preferably, or at least a check. Promises are like toilet paper, you need to flush that shit."

"I didn't ask for nothing because I don't want nothing. I'm here because—"

"See, you don't even know what you're doing. If you're here, you're supposed to be getting paid. That's the deal, my brother, and now, you know, Monster is done writing checks. Security is gone. He's on his own. So, you should have got yours when the getting was good."

"That's not who I am. I'm not always trying to get paid," I said.

Thug lifted an eyebrow. "Don't be selling me wolf tickets. We talked. You know the deal up here. I'm being straight with you so you don't have to talk that righteous bullshit with me."

"I appreciate that."

"No, you don't. But I don't really give a fuck if you do or not. See, I'm a free agent now. I ain't on nobody's payroll but my own."

"What? You're not working for Monster?"

"No, dog. I'm done. Monster's done. Rita's done and so are you. This shit is done."

Rita stood up and walked to the far end of the pool, staring at the fire in the distance.

"The fire is moving faster," she said.

She leaned against the railing; her long legs looked magnificent, her breasts perfect and natural. For having just had a baby, she was in beautiful shape.

Thug nodded toward Rita.

"Yeah, if I was into women, I'd be pimping that one. But no, my brother, she's yours, and yours to talk sense to. Monster paid me a lot of money to make sure you handled Rita, and if you can't, I was supposed to do whatever it takes to handle her, and you."

"Handle us?" I asked, still mesmerized by Rita.

"Stop looking at her. You got time enough for that, but you don't have much time to listen to what I have to tell you."

"What's that?"

Thug sat cross-legged and looked at me with that sardonic smile he always wore.

"I'm getting out. Today."

"Getting out? Why, I thought you had more money to wring out of Monster."

Thug stood and put on his pants, and shook his head as though he was through with me.

"Didn't I tell you? You must not have been listening."

"Listening to what?"

"I told you that someday Monster's house of cards would fall in. Today is that day."

"What, how?"

"Monster has always been nuts, but he's way nuts now, so soon as I get my shit together I'm bailing. I suggest you do too."

"If he's always been pretty fucking crazy, why are you giving up on him now?"

Thug sighed, shaking his head. "Look, I'll run it down one more time, you know, hit you upside the head with truth, but don't get stupid and start yelling and acting righteous like some dumb-ass white boy who thinks he invented morality."

This must be the truth because Thug never slipped out of character long enough to use a word like "morality."

"Listen to me because this is it, once you hear this it's on you. Monster wanted me to handle you."

"What does that mean?"

"Don't be stupid, my brother."

"He wants you to kill us?"

"'Handle you' means whatever it takes. Overdose you, make you disappear. Whatever."

"Did you do that to the boy?"

Thug looked at me with great pain in his eyes.

"You know, I could knock a fool out without a problem, I'm up for that, but I don't kill people who don't need killing. I ain't like that."

"I lucked out," I said.

"Maybe, but Monster got lots of folks on his payroll who don't have the scruples I got."

"So, you think they'll do it, hurt her or me?"

"Oh, hell, yeah! You need to know that."

"Who do you mean?"

"One of them is that Sheriff Graves. Now that mutha-fucka needs to die. Don't you even look in his direction; he's nothing but a corrupt cracker with a badge. You better be glad you never pushed the panic button on that pager he gave you."

"You knew about that pager?"

"Of course, I was the one who gave it to him, on orders from Monster."

"What would have happened to me?"

"Your ass would have been disappeared like Manny."

"Is that what happened to him?"

"What do you think? See, you got to know how this game is played. Monster is tying up all the loose ends so he can keep what he wants: money and the baby. Everything else can burn as far as that fool is concerned and he's willing to pay for it."

"You think he set those fires?"

Thug shrugged. "I don't know, but I wouldn't put it past him."

Then I felt a chill run through me: What had happened to Asha?

"What about Asha and Bridget?"

Thug shrugged and wrapped a towel around his bald head like a turban.

"That I don't know, my brother. Maybe they cut the right deal with Monster and they got out."

"Why are you telling me this?"

Thug smiled and walked over and patted me on the shoulder.

"Because I got all the money I need and I'm sick of being Monster's nigga, tired of being his thug, and he should pay for all the shit he did."

I believed him, though I don't know why. Then, as he walked away, Thug turned and gave me a nod.

"Monster is tripping, big time. He's never been what you call rational, but now he's got serious delusion going on, Jim Jones kind of delusion. Watch your back, my brother."

Thug was gone, and later in the day, when I was back at the bungalow, I saw him tooling downhill in the Maybach, getting out while the getting was good, a black man of means.

RITA HAD ME FOLLOW HER to her apartment in the farthest-flung region of the mansion, the part of the Lair where the important guests were lodged. She didn't seem at all bothered by Thug's take on everything, but it did make me think that I was crazy coming back here, that I should have taken the money and run. And it was hard to ignore the thickening white ash falling like snow, portending the fire next time was here. Rita changed into black sweats and running shoes, pulled her hair back into a tight bun, and looked determined and ready for whatever.

I looked out of the window and saw people gathered near the road: the gardening crew, cooks, and house cleaners boarding vans to leave the Lair. Near the Ferris wheel a fire engine waited for the encroaching fire with its exhausted crew sprawled out on the lawn.

"How do you think Monster feels about abandoning the Lair?"

"How do you know he's going anywhere? He could stay here, living in the tunnels below, like some fucking rodent," she said, with a face red with anger. "Monster thought he could get rid of me with money or lawyers, with Thug and with you, but I'm not going away. I'm right here until I get my baby back. I don't care if this whole sick world burns down."

She yanked out a drawer, turned it over and out, and pulled hard at something taped to the bottom. She came up with a small silver gun that seemed very big in her hand.

"What are you going to do?" I asked.

"You don't need to know that. What I need you to do is go with me."

"Where?"

"To get my baby back."

I had to laugh. She must have thought I was Superman, or maybe in her mind she was Superwoman. Either way, it was a stupid idea.

"Rita, the best thing you can do is get out of here and get yourself a lawyer. You'll get a settlement; you'll get your baby back. It's obvious that Monster is crazy, and any sane judge isn't going to give him custody of the baby."

Rita stood up.

"I'm asking for your help to do something that needs to be done. I'm not asking for your advice, I'm asking you to go with me in there and help me."

"What good is that going to do? Monster will have me arrested as soon as I step in there. It's different for you. You're his wife, he can't have you arrested for trespassing, for taking your baby. That's not kidnapping for you. For me that's life in prison."

She scowled in my direction.

"You don't know what I'm up against. When a judge finds you mentally incompetent, you don't have shit to say when it comes to your baby."

"Okay, but still, how are we going to get this done?"

"I know things about the Lair that Monster doesn't know."

"I don't know if this makes sense. We can figure out a better way of doing this."

"Don't be a fucking coward. Stand for something."

"I'm not a fucking coward and fuck you for calling me one."

"Monster isn't going to hurt you. He's not a Saturday-morning-cartoon villain. Show some courage."

"I have courage, but I've got to use my common sense; otherwise I'm a fool."

"Did Monster get into your mind with his mumbo jumbo? Did he scare you?"

"What are you talking about? Monster's got a small army of idiots in uniforms to protect him."

Rita laughed, and she looked a bit like the woman I remembered weeks ago.

"You just haven't been here long enough. You get used to this, this craziness."

I wished I could be like her, sure that if we charged into Monster's Lair, something good could come of it.

"Monster did something to me. Something, I don't understand, but it fucked my head. I saw things last time I was there. I can't remember what happened, but I catch glimpses, images."

"Monster does do things to you. He's good at that. He has all the drugs that no one else has. He's got this Hong Kong chemist who cooks them up for him. You hallucinate, speed up, and crash."

"I heard about this chemist, Mr. Chow. He's another good reason for me not to be in there."

"Here," she said, and unzipped her fanny pack, and took out the silver-plated .22. She tried to hand me the gun, but I backed away.

"No, I don't want it."

"Take it, if it's going to give you confidence."

"I'll throw it in the trash," I said, and she put the gun back in her fanny pack.

"No, you won't. I worked like hell smuggling that thing in here."

"I'm not going to shoot Monster. I'm a lot of things, but not a murderer."

"I need your help, that's all. I'm not asking you to shoot anybody. I just need you to be there for me. It'll be easy."

"If it's so easy, why didn't you take the baby earlier?"

"Because Monster did something to my head. I couldn't stand up to him, one person can't stand up to him, but together we can. We can make him respect us, put the fear of God in him."

"You think?" I said, shaking my head with doubt.

"I know. I know it for a fact, we can do this."

Rita rushed the door as if she had been waiting for the right moment to burst free from the confines of the room with me following at her heels.

"Hurry!" she said, and I did my best, but she was quick and fit and I was a winded, out-of-shape cook.

I thought that since we were inside the Lair, the mansion proper, it wouldn't be a big deal to head over to Monster's wing. I wasn't sure I would go with her; this wasn't my problem, and it seemed suicidal. Monster must have still had some Security in his employ, and if not them, Sheriff Graves might be about, and if he made Thug worry, the last thing I wanted was to see him again. I wanted to go, find my way down off the mountain ahead of the fire, but I followed her.

"There's no way we can get to Monster from the inside," she said. "But there's another way."

Hard wind blew from the north, the sky was red and black, and stinging sand whipped against my face.

"Come on, follow me," she said. We ran along a path that circled the mansion until we came to a heavy metal door. She didn't bother trying it, but I did. It was locked. I turned back to Rita, but she was gone, pulling herself up the wisteria-covered walls to a destination I didn't want to think about.

I hated heights.

She stopped fifty feet above the ground and stood up on a

ledge, holding on to the wall, reaching into the heavy foliage, pulling at something—an electrical box? I heard a click, and the metal door swung open. Rita climbed down quickly and waved for me to follow her inside. In the darkness we reached a stairwell, which we took to the bottom. There we were in a part of the mansion I hadn't seen before.

"We're past the grand hall and now we're at the living quarters."

Voices came from up ahead. She opened another door, and light flooded over us, the sun itself.

Blinded, I stumbled forward into a sweltering room, some kind of sauna. I heard voices and laughter. Finally my eyes adjusted enough for me to see.

There were maybe a half dozen blonds, naked and glistening with sweat, carrying water bottles that they shook and sprayed one another with. One gestured for us to follow.

"Ignore them, Monster's harem. They're so high, they're barely human."

I tried to avoid the boy, but he came toward me and grabbed onto my arm.

"Hey, get back!"

The boy ignored my command and rubbed himself against me. I shoved him down to the floor. Another boy approached and did the same thing, trying to rub up against me. I knocked him down and ran after Rita.

"How come they ignored you?" I asked her.

"I'm not a man," she said by way of an explanation.

After we crossed the hall, Rita's gun pointing the way, she opened another door that led to a cavernous space, dark as a Texas highway at night except for a blazing fireplace. We had arrived at the library where I first saw Monster and the baby.

Rita ran for the fireplace, pressed a hidden lever, and the fireplace slid away, revealing another stairwell.

"This is it. We'll find Monster here."

We started down the steep and narrow stairs, again walking in darkness. We slowly and carefully maneuvered down to the landing, where she pushed the door open.

We were in a bedroom, and there was Monster, naked in the way people seemed to like to be at the Lair, stretched out on a gigantic bed, almost engulfed by the pregnant plushness of pillows. Everything in the room was white, white as Monster. We were in a nursery, but the baby was nowhere to be seen. I didn't want to see Monster naked, sensing that it would be dangerous to look; I would become stone or a pillar of salt at the sight of something mind-boggling, like a gang of tentacles writhing away where his manhood should be.

It was wrong to look. I could sense it, that the perversity of Monster was more than his Clarence Thomas–like attempt to racially obliterate himself, his need to maintain the illusion of marriage, his harem—all of it would be explained by the brutalization of his own flesh, proof that what he was willing to do to others was nothing compared to what he had done to himself.

But I couldn't resist; my eyes burned to see the mystery of his sex.

I glanced quickly as Rita tried to wake him from a stupor.

Monster had no genitalia, just something that looked like a brass-ringed hole.

"What is that?"

Rita ignored me and kept shaking at Monster's arm.

"Did he do that to himself? Did he have himself cut like that?"

"What did you expect?" Rita said as she turned back to Monster. "Where is my baby?" she repeatedly screamed into his uncomprehending face.

A flutter of movement, lips twitching.

Dazed, with eyes as red as blood, he tried to stand, teetered, and fell back onto the bed.

Rita slapped him, and he cried in short, hard sobs.

"Go away," he said. "Where's my Security?"

"It's over, Monster. The hills are on fire, everyone is evacuating."

Finally, she got through to him. Monster more or less came to his senses.

"Rita, you are so wrong. I did so much for you, and you betray me, just like everybody else. Like those liars out there who talk about me like I'm some kind of child molester. You know the truth; I'm incapable of hurting anyone."

He glanced down at where his genitals should have been.

I felt like throwing up.

"Where is my baby?" Rita demanded.

"He's not yours. He's my flesh and blood."

"He's not, you fucking liar! He doesn't have an ounce of your blood in him, and if you don't tell me where he is, I'll shoot you down right now," she said, shoving the gun into his face.

Monster shoved the gun aside and ran to an armoire and flung it open to reveal an array of bottles with colored fluids inside.

"Leave those bottles alone. You're not poisoning me again."

Monster's hand darted for something among those dozens of multicolored containers.

Rita fired.

A red bottle slipped from his startled grasp and shattered on the floor. Whatever it was sizzled and evaporated into wisps of smoke. Immediately, I coughed and tasted pomegranates.

"Don't breathe!" Rita shouted to me as she dragged Monster into the hallway. I followed, eyes stinging and throat burning, only able to take a breath once the door closed behind us.

"Where is the baby?" she demanded of Monster as he crumpled on the cold slate of the hallway.

"The baby is home. He's safe at home," Monster replied.

"He'd never be safe with you. Give him to me," Rita said, and I was sure she would kill Monster.

"He's away from you. You'll never have him," Monster said, and started to shimmer and pulsate, skin churning, slipping into something else.

"Stop!"

Monster's face began to elongate into a snout, and that's when she shot him.

He continued to change and she continued to shoot until the gun clicked.

Too late.

Monster had become a massive wolflike creature, with bloody welts across its face. With a snarl, he padded away from us.

## VEGAN PINEAPPLE-SAFFRON UPSIDE-DOWN CAKE

TOPPING

5 tablespoons Earth Balance spread
½ cup plus 2 teaspoons raw brown sugar
1 pineapple

CAKE

2½ cups all-purpose flour
½ teaspoon baking powder
½ teaspoon baking soda
¼ teaspoon cardamom
¾ cup raw sugar
1 teaspoon salt
1 teaspoon saffron threads
½ cup water
⅔ cup coconut milk
5 tablespoons grapeseed oil

*Make the topping:* Put the Earth Balance spread and the brown sugar in a small saucepan and stir over medium heat until the spread has melted and the sugar has dissolved. Continue cooking, without stirring, for a few more minutes or until bubbles start to appear around the outside edges of the mixture and the sugar starts to caramelize. Then remove from the heat, and pour into a nonstick or sprayed 9-inch round cake pan.

Peel and slice the pineapple and arrange the slices evenly over the topping in the pan.

*Make the cake:* Preheat the oven to 350°F.

Sift the flour, baking powder, baking soda, and ground cardamom into a bowl. Place the sugar and salt on top of them and mix together. Take some of this dry mixture and, using a spice grinder, blend it with the saffron threads until you can no longer see any strands.

Using a whisk, combine the water, coconut milk, and grapeseed oil in a bowl. In thirds, add the wet mixture to the dry mixture and combine after each addition until you have a homogeneous batter. Pour the batter over the topping in the pan.

Bake at 350°F for 35 to 40 minutes. Cool completely, then invert onto a cake plate so that the pineapple slices are on top.

# CHAPTER NINE

"WE ARE HALLUCINATING," I SAID TO RITA calmly as she walked about in circles.

"No, he is some kind of thing. He does that. He's capable of anything!"

"Should I have said, Are we hallucinating?"

"He's a demon. A godforsaken thing."

"I don't know about you, but I think I'm going to faint," I said, and meandered away.

I found Monster's bathroom and washed my face, and dried it on a towel so thick I could plunge myself into it, submerging totally into the whiteness, its abundance, and wondered if a flock of geese would burst forth.

I returned to her with the towel wrapped around my head.

"I can taste it. It's bitter and thick on my tongue. Don't you taste it? We're both very high," I said with satisfaction.

"What are you talking about? That man has my child, he turned into some werewolf thing and I shot him and it didn't do anything."

"I've been very drunk. I've smoked hashish, chewed peyote, done acid, ecstasy, but I've never felt this."

"Shut up!"

"Listen. My heart, I can feel the beat reverberating throughout my body. The blood rushes all around me, flowing from me into the air around us."

I meant every word I said because I wanted Rita to know Monster wasn't really a monster but a freak who had thrown us all into a poisoned river.

Rita pointed the gun at my head, gesturing for me to shut up.

"If you say another word . . . I swear to God I will shoot you."

I made the sign for dreaming. *We're in a dream*, I signed over and over again until she lost interest at pointing the gun at my head.

"You don't think he's a werewolf?"

"No."

"Good," she said. "Let's go kill him."

I nodded and followed her to a passageway that led to a corridor that stretched for what seemed like a mile.

"Where is it that we're going?"

"Home! Where the baby is," she said.

"Where is that?"

She ignored me and pulled away. I did my best to keep up with her, but again it was hopeless. Comfortable running at a near sprint, Rita must have been in training for this. I had nothing left, and resigned myself to walking.

I heard something behind me, faint like the rustling of leaves, then a deep-throated growl. I found renewed energy to continue running, saw an open door glowing like a light to the next world.

"Hurry!" Rita yelled from the doorway.

That sound behind me now was a roar of anguish.

Fear picked up my feet, lifted my knees, pumped my arms, filled my lungs; I flung myself forward as if I was at the tape at the end of a race and stumbled through the doorway. Rita slammed the heavy metal door behind me, and soon afterward something struck it, growling and thrashing.

It was a relief to be aboveground and to feel the cooler air coming off the ocean, but from the northeast, as far as I could see, everything was on fire.

"Come on," Rita said. But I stood there, astonished at the approaching destruction and the sound of it, the explosions.

"That's Monster's Lair going up," Rita said over her shoulder as she headed to the bluffs. She knew where she was going, but I hoped it didn't involve trying to climb down a steep cliff onto the rocks below.

"Over here," she said.

I was certain now that Monster had bought all this property for just this kind of contingency, the need for avenues of escape.

She walked along a worn, narrow trail bordered on both sides by clover and wildflowers. The path gently sloped into a forest of oaks, and in the center was a high stone wall, and behind the wall, a picture-perfect cottage looking as if it should have been made of gingerbread. There, half concealed by giant hollyhocks, oblivious to the ash floating about, stood a big-boned woman with intricately braided blond hair. Behind her on the ground in a wicker baby basket was a squawking, red-faced little blond boy.

The woman saw us coming and scooped up the boy and disappeared into the house. She returned clutching a shotgun.

"Stop! You are trespassing," she said in heavily accented English.

"Who are you?" Rita asked.

"You are trespassing!"

"Listen! I want my baby!"

Heidi didn't seem to understand Rita, or maybe she did because she pointed the shotgun at her.

"Let me explain it to you. That's my baby and you will have to kill me to stop me from taking him."

Rita started down the path past the huge hollyhocks, the great sunflowers, the trellis covered with the butter-yellow blossoms of a climbing rose to the quaint, artfully painted *Home* on the wooden gate.

The woman fired the shotgun, and the baby wailed. Rita dropped to the ground and crawled for cover behind a blooming jacaranda tree.

I didn't have cover to hide behind. I stood there, hands at my sides, expecting to be shot. I imagined being ripped apart by the pellets, bleeding to death on a bed of primrose. I didn't care; she could shoot me, kill me, I didn't care. The baby and Rita, that's what mattered, but the woman wasn't interested in me. She calmly positioned herself to get a better shot at Rita.

I picked up a good-size stone and hit her flush in the back.

She moved the barrel of the shotgun in my direction. Rita rushed her and hit the woman in the head with the butt of the gun, knocking her to the ground, and scooped up the baby.

I grabbed the shotgun from the grasping hands of the woman and followed after Rita and the baby. With the baby pressed against her chest, Rita flew down narrow wooden stairs that led to a small dock and to a motorboat anchored there.

I untied the motorboat and climbed on board.

"I've never piloted a ship," I said.

"I have. We're going to Santa Barbara. I have friends there."

"Monster can find you. You need a shelter, someplace he can't get to. Asha can find you a shelter. She'll know how to get you free from Monster."

Rita laughed. "Don't need to worry about me. I don't intend to run from Monster. I want all this. I want everything he has, and I will get it, and that still won't be enough for what he's done."

Rita hopped onto the boat, placed the baby inside the cabin; that's when I saw the black figure of the giant dog running headfirst down the bluffs.

"Start the engine!" I shouted to Rita.

It took a long frantic moment or two for the engine to engage, long enough for the giant dog to land on the dock.

I grabbed the shotgun and aimed. The dog leaped and I fired. I was sure I'd hit it, but the dog kept coming, undeterred and pissed, too close for me to get off another shot. I swung with the stock and whiffed.

The dog lunged, knocking the shotgun from my hands, and sank its teeth into my shoulder and, with a yank, flung me off the boat and onto the dock.

Rita rushed to face it, but it was on her in a flash, throwing her about viciously.

I expected that it would tear her head from her shoulders, but unexpectedly it stopped and gazed at the sky.

The sun, a gaudy reddish balloon, had risen above the haze, and the dog continued to stare at it, as though compelled.

The dog coughed as dogs sometimes do, and lowered its head and opened its mouth wide until it became a gaping maw. It coughed hard and vomited prodigiously, and something long and black slid from within it, and then the dog was gone and there was Monster, wet and steaming as if he had just slipped from out of the womb, but his blinding white skin was gone. Monster was black now, black as a shadow. Black like the trespasser who he complained had stalked him all those years.

I thought Monster was done, that the drugs had worn off; the gig was up.

No.

Monster was still possessed with the need to kill Rita.

"You bitch. You hateful bitch! After all I did for you, you stab me in the back! What were you before I came and pulled you from the mud? You fucking trailer trash!"

Monster had the build and the strength of an anorexic, but his ego was oversize.

He charged Rita.

With one punch she knocked him to the deck and began to beat him with all the unrepressed energy of someone freed from bondage.

"The baby! The baby is crying," I shouted, hoping to

coax her off of Monster, but she seemed intent on bashing his head in.

"Stop it, Rita. You can't be killing people," Thug shouted.

I glanced up to see Thug walking down the stairs, smiling as though this insanity was a pleasant night at the club.

I picked up the shotgun and pointed it at him, but he didn't seem concerned.

He lifted Monster from the deck, cradled him as though he was the frailest child.

"Monster isn't all that. Y'all treat him like he's the one, the devil or some shit. Sure, he's done some really wrong shit, but you know, he don't deserve this. He don't deserve to die. He's done some good too. You know that. And he gave me another retainer and met my number."

"You can talk, Thug, but he didn't steal your baby," Rita said, anger erupting in her voice.

Thug smiled easily.

"Please, Rita. Don't act like you the innocent victim. Your ass signed on with Monster just like everybody else. You wanted to get paid and you got paid. You a rich woman and you'll be a rich woman all your life because of Monster. You just wanted it all, just like all you white people; you want it all, not just your fair share. You want it all."

Thug turned and started up the stairs with Monster.

"Where are you going with him?" I asked.

"Away. Monster isn't gonna be judged by these fools.

Maybe the Congo. He likes the monkeys and elephants. Yeah, maybe the Congo or Poland. They love him in Poland. Plenty of blonds in Poland."

Thug gave one last disarming smile and with a shrug disappeared into the smoke and haze of the burning world.

## FLOURLESS GLUTEN-FREE CHOCOLATE TORTE

SUGAR TOPPING

Confectioners' sugar, as needed
Instant coffee powder, as needed

CAKE

6 egg yolks
1 egg
⅓ cup plus 2 tablespoons sugar
1 cup butter
2 cups dark chocolate morsels
13 egg whites

*Make the topping:* Use equal parts of confectioners' sugar and instant coffee powder, enough to dust the finished torte. Blend the sugar and coffee in a food processor or spice grinder until well combined. Set aside.

*Make the cake:* Prepare molds or a cake pan by spraying with Pam, lining with parchment paper, and then spraying again with Pam. Preheat the oven to 325°F.

In a mixer bowl fitted with the wire attachment, whip the egg yolks, egg, and 2 tablespoons sugar for 7 minutes; pour into another bowl and set aside. Melt the butter and chocolate morsels in the microwave or over a double boiler; set aside, keeping warm. Clean the mixer bowl and the wire attachment. Put the egg whites and 1/3 cup sugar in the mixer bowl and, using the wire attachment, whip to make a meringue with medium-stiff peaks. Do not overwhip.

Whisk the warm chocolate mixture into the egg-yolk mixture. Do not allow the chocolate to set. Quickly but gently, fold in the meringue. Pour into the prepared molds or pan. Bake at 325°F for 12 to 15 minutes. The torte should be slightly gooey in the center but not liquid. Cool it in the refrigerator to set it before turning it out of the pan.

Put the coffee sugar in a sieve and dust it over the chilled torte.

# CHAPTER TEN

LAST I HEARD RITA HAD BECOME ONE OF the richest women in Santa Barbara County; even after all the lawsuits she was worth easily a hundred million. She lived in even more seclusion than she had before with Monster, but she was as discreet as Monster was outrageous, living behind high walls in the cottage near the ocean that Monster had used as a day care center for the boy. She never had Monster's Lair rebuilt. Instead, she sold the land to another über-entertainer who fancied herself queen of the world.

I visited Rita once, at her request, to have her sign papers in person for our business venture before I returned east.

I didn't know what to expect because I'd heard the press and the lawyers representing those boys, the blond automatons, had descended on her, ready to tear her to shreds as the inheritor of Monster's fortune. Supposedly, Monster died in the great Santa Ynez fire, and all those allegations of child endangerment, murder, and uncategorizable perversity vanished with him. As Thug would have said, it was all good. Far as the world knew, Monster's sins had been burned away, cleansed by his horrible death, and fans returned to his catalog with renewed passion.

Bullshit as that was, it wasn't up to me to get the record straight that Monster had not died but had escaped with his freedom and much of his fortune.

Anyway, Rita handled the aftermath expertly. She settled with everyone who had a claim and wanted to settle; and those who didn't she sicced the dogs on, producing documentation, proof that the parents were pimping their kids to Monster.

It was always about the money.

Rita knew the score, so she walled herself away with the same rings of concentric security that Monster had. Her Security crew didn't look like Mormons in jumpsuits but like locals: jeans and cowboy boots, Lakers caps and cell phones pressed against their ears.

Her little boy played in the idyllic English cottage garden, chasing butterflies. Rita came out of the house with a glass of lemonade for me and kissed my cheek. Now that the troubles of Monster were over for her, she wore her hair long and had gained some weight, and looked the better for it: a beautiful, relaxed woman who had everything she needed in this world and the next.

"You look wonderful, as beautiful as the first time I saw you, when you pretended that you couldn't speak."

She laughed.

"I probably couldn't. I was too depressed to say anything to anyone."

"You don't have to do this," I said to her as I opened my briefcase and brought out the numerous papers that needed her signature.

"Yes, I want to. You helped me get my boy back."

I watched as Rita, my silent partner, signed the paperwork for the lease on a restaurant on the Lower East Side that would mark my return to the restaurant world.

"You know, I heard something about Monster."

"You should call the police," I said, alarmed.

"No, there's no need. He's changed."

"How's that?"

"I guess it's not that big of a change. He's no longer a man, if he ever was. He's a woman now. And he runs a children's theater in Poland."

"Jesus! He must make one ugly-looking woman. Have you seen a picture?"

"No. I'm not that interested."

"So, it all worked out. Monster has his freedom and the

youth of Poland to work with, and you have what you need, and I have a restaurant to run," I said.

"Yes," she replied. "How is it with your wife?"

"It's good and she's pregnant."

"You're a lucky man to have something to go home to."

"Yes, I do feel lucky. Everything worked out the way it should have. We're lucky people."

I didn't mention my struggle to control my drug addiction. I guess all the trouble with Monster started all that up again, though it was always there, right below the surface. Elena recognized that now and helped me stay sober, keeping an eye on me as if at any moment I might fly away like a wayward pigeon finding his way back to the cocaine roost. But I wouldn't let that happen. I would hold on to this life, this good life, never turning it loose. Elena was with me; I could hold on to her at night, feel her swelling belly, and I'd rather die than lose what I had with her.

"Yeah, we've been very lucky, fortunate or whatever you want to call it."

"Isn't it lovely to think so?" Rita said as she looked out at the beautiful world Monster had made possible for her, as the baby cried forlornly, snatching at butterflies too far from his grasp.

# ACKNOWLEDGMENTS

I'D LIKE TO THANK MY MOM, LOLITA Teresa Villavaso, who's given me much love and material to write about, and my dad, Hillary Louis Tervalon, who took me to the beach or the park or anywhere else I ever wanted to go when I was an indulged boy. I want to thank my lovely, brilliant daughters, Giselle and Elise, who like to eat my cooking and never wash a dish; and Sammy, my stepson, the little naked boy from Shanghai. I want to thank his mom too, for bringing all that happiness with her, and it's hard to thank Mary Blodgett and Carlton Calvin enough for hosting our wonderful wedding reception, and for their perpetual kindness. I need to thank my buddy JGold from way, way back, back beyond that—getting handcuffed with you on Beverly Boulevard was a laugh because LAPD didn't shoot us—and Tracy Sherrod, my Goddess Editor, so glad to be back with you. My thanks to Jon Gray, Malcolm Livingston, and Lester Walker, with respect and admiration for what you do and what you all bring to the table.

And I need to thank my crew of misanthropes and disreputable types: Mr. Eric Chow, Mr. Tim Stiles, Mr. J. Michael Walker, Mr. Bernard Ng, Mr. Ed Webb, Mr. Andrew Ramirez, and my friends from back in the CCS days, Bob Blaisdell, Max and Elaine Schott, Caroline Allen, and Elizabeth Wong from the Disney Screenwriting days. Robin Tiffney—thanks for the advice and cookies. And lastly, Biscuit, for helping me get in shape and for the pleasure of picking up his droppings each and every day.

## ABOUT THE AUTHOR

JERVEY TERVALON is the author of five books, including the bestselling *Dead Above Ground* and *Understand This*, for which he won the New Voices Award from the Quality Paperback Book Club. He edited the anthology *The Cocaine Chronicles.* He was a Remsen Bird writer in residence at Occidental College and a Disney screenwriting fellow. He is the director of the *Literature for Life* project, an online literary magazine and salon, and the literary director of LitFest Pasadena. Born in New Orleans, he now lives in California and teaches at the College of Creative Studies at UC Santa Barbara.

## ABOUT THE CHEFS

CHEF LESTER WALKER hails from Co-Op City in the North Bronx. While at the School of Food and Finance, he became inspired to feed his culinary passion and won a C-CAP cooking competition, which awarded him with a scholarship to Johnson & Wales University. His skills place him among the best chefs in the country, as evidenced by his Food Network *Chopped* win. You can catch Chef Lester melting faces as one of the founding chefs of Ghetto Gastro.

CHEF MALCOLM LIVINGSTON II is a Bronx native. After graduating from the former Culinary Art Institute of New York City, he became the youngest kitchen staff member at Sirio Maccioni's Le Cirque. After making his rounds among New York City's elite dining institutions, Malcolm landed a post at wd~50, where he continues to lead innovation as the pastry chef. He is listed among *Dessert Professional*'s 2013 Top Ten and a 2014 James Beard Rising Star Chef nominee. Chef Malcolm is a founding member of the Ghetto Gastro culinary collective.